T0157003

PANSY'S CHEST

Christiana T Moronfolu

Pansy's Chest

Christiana .T. Moronfolu

Order this book online at www.trafford.com
or email orders@trafford.com

Most Trafford titles are also available at major online book retailers.

COVER DESIGN BY
Tolic Arts, Baton Of Love Ventures
batonoflove_ventures@yahoo.com

Print information available on the last page.

ISBN: 978-1-4907-9001-5 (sc)
ISBN: 978-1-4907-9007-7 (e)

Trafford rev. 08/15/2018

www.trafford.com
North America & international
toll-free: 1 888 232 4444 (USA & Canada)
fax: 812 355 4082

Dedication

To the King Of Love, the Shepherd of romance be all adoration. His goodness truly doesn't fail. With Him is all you want in a relationship; natal or conjugal. His splendour can be seen in the beauty of the tapestry of nations and kingdoms woven together, praising Him in resound of His works in the lives of the children of men. I appreciate all my family and friends from the diverse cultures and works of life.

PANSY'S CHEST

This page is dedicated to my father,

Late Pa Jacob Mobolaji Moronfolu,

(17th December 1935 - 30th April 2018),

Who fell asleep while I was writing this book.

Your love for me through the help of God

Brought me this far.

I told you about this novel

I know you got excited for me

You were just not priviledge to stay

And see its conclusion.

Thank you daddy, enjoy your rest!

Chapter One

Cradles Of Intervention

Tiana sat in the garden in the cool of the day as Marie slept in her crib. She was the most beautiful baby Tiana had ever seen and her brother Chrysan looked just like her. Though she enjoyed the company of her twins, she looked forward to setting up Sanderstead Tiny Feet; a nursery for ages zero to five. Prior to delivery, she had been re-orientated with the operations of the Freeman Home and Garden while George and Rose diverted their energy to ensure smooth running of the business outside the home.

Dahlia Monk, the thirty five years old live in Spanish house keeper was very efficient in updating Tiana on the state of affairs in the home and Tiana gave the feedback to Rose and George. Prior to Tiana's arrival, Dahlia had combined her housekeeping role with the management of the garden. While Tiana comfortably managed the two roles in her previous trip, Dahlia struggled with them. The farm manager, Singh Raj had to step in and take on additional responsibilities of managing the garden to help Dahlia. Tiana's return to the Freeman's home was thus seen as a relief. Singh was able to step down and Tiana's role as administrator for the home and garden was reinstated. Unlike Tiana, Dahlia didn't need to go to school; she was more homely and loved to bake cakes.

The Freeman family also employed an eighteen year old Rita Smart as a live out nanny to assist with Chrysan and Marie. Rita lived down the street and worked from seven o'clock in the mornings to seven o'clock in the evenings. She was such an extrovert, that she insisted on taking the children out daily. She enjoyed pushing the twin pram and buggy to the local library, which was a ten minute bus ride away. While Marie appeared to enjoy the baby sessions at the library on Tuesdays, Chrysan had his moments. On days they were not in the library, she took them to Sanderstead Activity Group for an hour. This was a drop in charity set up by the government that allowed children to drop in and play for up to one hour daily. Tiana enjoyed the company of Rita because she was a very chatty lady. She also had the opportunity to learn more about the British culture from Rita.

Jayden spent the summer evening in the oval artificial pool with his family before Marie began to show signs of distress and had to be taken out of the water. Chrysan giggled as Jayden splashed water on him. He was more playful and energetic than his sister, ate twice as much as she did and practically stayed awake all day. While Marie slept with ease and with little persuasion, Chrysan had to be rocked to sleep. He was given a shower every night, had his body massaged with oil and stretched before he could sleep at night.

Tiana was once again lost in her thoughts, for the past six years had left a strain on her emotions. She knew what it was to have a dashed hope and bruised ego. Her marriage to Jayden had been a cradle of intervention to what could have been a disastrous end to her love life. She occasionally had flash backs on her previous trip to the Freeman's and only came round when she heard the children or Jayden.

Sometimes she had doubts about her sense of belonging; constantly experiencing cultural shock; life was as different as an outsider. She had recently been grafted into the Freeman Home and had quite a lot to learn. The Freeman Home and Garden was hers and her children served as another cradle of intervention to what would have been a lonely marriage. Though married to Jayden, the past events were still vivid in her memory but the children's constant demands kept her from drowning in her thoughts. She would never have guessed the end from the beginning. The recent years' events had overtaken her emotions and she realised that she had got married before sorting out her feelings. She had to learn to love and trust genuinely again. The peaceful look on Marie's face as she slept and the light giggles from Chrysan once again assured her that she had made the right move.

At twenty nine, apart from overseeing the Freeman Home and Garden, she also looked after her twins and husband. George and Rose began their day by inspecting the Freeman Garden daily. Next they went and volunteered in the local church for two hours before visiting Dora. They return home for lunch and siesta and in the evenings, they went to socialise at the bar in Croham Park bed and breakfast.

Tiana lived with her family in the five bedroom cottage attached to a half acre garden, sectioned by hedges in Sanderstead. The cottage is assessable through a patio garden from the narrow street which isn't motorable. Cars were packed on adjacent streets. The Freeman family had one car; a van that delivered the garden produce to the market and supplied nearby commercial outlets with dairy products. The cottage had an exit door at its rear that led to the lawn which opened up to the north garden.

The north garden was where the four dairy cows were bred and milked daily from spring to autumn. A portion of the north garden was sectioned off and used for grooming the two horses. George and Rose enjoyed horse riding for many years, even before they got married. The east garden was used for poultry, fish pond and rabbits' hutch and the west garden was used to cultivate fruits and vegetables. The oval artificial pool and garden seat were positioned on the lawn at the rear garden.

The cottage next door belonged to the Jacks, who ran a respite centre; Jack + Sons Home. This was Dora's care home and on his return to the UK, Jayden worked there voluntarily. For Tiana, Jack + Sons served as another cradle of intervention for Jayden to return to the UK and re-integrate with the system after thirty years. 24th April, 2018.

Prior to her marriage, Tiana had grown up in a care home. OCHS also known as Oluremilekun Children's Home, Sagamu, Ogun State had served as the first cradle of intervention that helped shape Tiana's life. Though encouraged to mingle with other children, she chose to live a restrictive life. She subjected herself to a secluded lifestyle and always reached out to learn and grow. Deep within she felt that she was destined for greatness so she didn't compare herself with the other children in the home. This fuelled her strong desire to reach out to the world beyond her.

PANSY'S CHEST

Back at OCHS, a school bus was arranged to take all the ladies to their nearby schools and bring them back. The infant, junior and high schools were all within twenty five minutes drive from the home. The home also arranged supervised group visits to places of interest. OCHS aimed to offer the children ages zero to nineteen years old a comprehensive care that catered for the total child. By the age of eighteen, they were expected to have learnt how to be independent of the home, hence were allowed to go to town at week ends.

The religious needs of the girls below eighteen were met within the home. While muslim ladies above eighteen were allowed to attend the masjid in town on Fridays, the Christian ladies above eighteen were allowed to attend the chapel in town on Sundays. On Saturdays all the ladies above eighteen were encouraged to go to the public library as well as the market in town. They were also encouraged to be industrious and they made their money by offering their services within the home. Their main trades were catering, hair dressing, tailoring and arts and crafts. It was also during their eighteenth year that they took their entrance examinations into the university.

By the age of nineteen, it was expected of the ladies to gain admission into a tertiary institution, study part time and work or be fully engaged in a vocational trade. More so, on their departure from the home at nineteen, each received a settlement package. This served as a cradle of intervention to curb poverty and other social vices among the ladies when they left OCHS.

Although wealthy individuals were allowed to sponsor children in OCHS, they were made to sign an undertaking to allow all ladies at the age of nineteen walk away without any obligations, on receipt of their settlement package; a maintenance subsidy of three hundred thousand naira each. The only condition was that they got a placement either in the tertiary institution or on a vocational trade before they left OCHS. This didn't affect their rights to work with their sponsors. Should they apply for job vacancies, they were treated fairly and subjected to the same screening exercise as the other job applicants.

Chapter Two

A Flavour Of love

The strong desire for success was evident in all Tiana's relationships as she came across as being too intimidating for the local boys. At eighteen, Tiana began dating the local boys in Iperu Akesan Bale Oja, a town in Ogun State. OCHS opened her gates from twelve noon to seven o'clock in the evenings on Fridays to Sundays. Her first date, eighteen years old Kolapo Andrews, was a tall, dark and rich popular Iperu teenager in Iperu High School. His date with Tiana ended when she couldn't control her appetite.

On a couple of outings to the eateries in Iperu on Saturdays,

PANSY'S CHEST

Tiana had ordered food in large proportions, ate what she could and taken the rest back to the OCHS. The shy Kolapo was always too intimidated to ask her to share the food he bought. He was also forced to maintain a one sided conversation, whenever they went out because Tiana hardly responded to him rather she focussed on her needs.

On their last outing, Kolapo ordered five large pieces of meat pies, six large sausage rolls, four large jam doughnuts, two medium sized ring doughnuts, four medium fairy sponge cakes and four medium sized bottles of soft drinks. As usual Tiana asked for a takeaway bag and packed the food and drinks inside. As she ate the food, he told her that the food smelt nice and spicy, expecting Tiana to offer him some. She failed to get the hint and after the meal, Kolapo quietly drifted away. He stopped meeting her in town and refused to pick her calls or respond to her messages.

Her friends in OCHS soon noticed she stopped bringing food home on Saturdays and she informed them that she had stopped dating Kolapo. According to her, he was a loud guy who loved to spend money but was of little brain. Kolapo also left Tiana because of several unethical stunts she pulled on him while on other social outings. They dated for only five months.

Her next boyfriend was Dandy Omojuola, a twenty seven year old car mechanic she met two months after leaving Kolapo. Although Dandy dropped out of school after form three, he was also a socialite in Iperu and he didn't mind Tiana's appetite initially. Dandy was very vocal, unlike Kolapo. It was whilst they were dating that he cautioned her about eating alone when they both went out. He also taught her to mind her orders and stop taking extras home. Just before her nineteenth birthday, Tiana got her university admission. Dandy got excited and decided to borrow his friend's car, a Toyota Camry to take Tiana to the club on Saturday afternoon to celebrate. Whilst at the club they all danced, drank and chatted with one another. Switching of dance partners was encouraged and Tiana went back to the children's home in a Lexus jeep.

PANSY'S CHEST

A banker she met at the club talked her into going back to OCHS with him after dancing. This made Dandy very angry and he broke up with her. Tiana had other social flaws that convinced Dandy that she was not right for him. They dated for about five months. Tiana on the other hand wanted an educated boyfriend like Patrick Chike, the banker that took her home. She never saw Patrick again after he dropped her at OCHS.

After dancing with her, Patrick had cajoled her into going into his Lexus jeep where he smooched and kissed her passionately. After a while, he dropped her off at OCHS and this wetted Tiana's appetite for stronger men. In a couple of weeks she would be off to University of Lagos to pursue a career in social health care. She believed that was where life was and that was where she would dig for her gold and diamond jewels! Friday 11th July, 2008.

Tiana was a very beautiful lady with her ebony complexion, six foot height and robust build. She had very long curly blonde hair that reached her Venus fold. The most striking feature in Tiana were her hazel eyes and the glow of her blonde hair. Besides that she had large and sparkling white eyeballs, a pointed nose and sumptuous lips that made her looks so enchanting. Her sharp penetrating looks and captivating presence couldn't be missed as she stood head and shoulder above her peers. She was a delight to behold but her only challenge was that she was very rustic and crude; lacking the basic social skills.

This was later attributed to the restricted life style she had adopted from her early years in the children's home. On receipt of her three hundred thousand settlement package, Tiana bade farewell to OCHS and headed for her university. Before gaining admission, she had applied for a part time role and was offered the position of a shop assistant in a retail outlet near the university. During the week of her registration, she met three friends on campus; Chioma Etti, Habiba Mohammed and Ewaoluwa Tolulope. They all agreed to rent a flat together in Onike, Yaba Lagos.

As a fresher, she quickly made a name for herself as an

unethical flirt. She had been known in the clubs and bars around school. Luckily, she managed to preserve her virginity, one thing she vowed to reserve for her man, the one she would marry. By the end of the year, her name appeared in the school magazine, as 'a girl momma mustn't meet' and she also bagged the award for 'every guy's nightmare'. This negative publicity humiliated her so she stopped dating, hence her second and third years were silent years on campus.

At the start of her final year, her friends encouraged her to go back into dating and after several failed attempts at securing a steady date, she got into online dating through the influence of her friends. At the age of twenty one she had sown her wild oats and learnt a great deal of lesson in dating. She knew by the time she graduated the following year, she would need a man to settle down with. Tiana finally met a British guy online who lived in Sanderstead. They chatted for about a year online and seemed to get along well; laughing and exchanging pictures and video clips. Hubert Knight promised to marry her after her National Youth Service year. Throughout the relationship, he sent her flowers, gifts and money. She soon became the envy of her friends Habiba, Ewaoluwa and Chioma.

At the age of twenty two, she graduated and was posted to do her National Youth Service in a health centre in Surulere Lagos. This meant that she could retain her accommodation in Yaba. OCHS had shut her doors to Tiana, so she had to fend for herself. Her monthly salary of twenty five thousand naira was barely enough so Hubert came to rescue her and augmented it with an additional twenty five thousand naira.

Tiana's friends Habiba and Chioma were posted to serve outside Lagos and Ewaoluwa who recently completed her masters program had already done her youth service. This meant that Tiana had to share the Onike flat with other university students, as they needed it. The four friends kept in touch regularly, exchanging their online dating experiences and encouraging one another. Only Tiana seemed to have won the jackpot of a steady online date. Upon completion of her service year, Hubert proposed to Tiana online and sent her the ring by post. Everyone was delighted and Tiana's love tale finally became the envy of her friends and colleagues at work.

By the time she was 'passing out' at the end of her service year, Hubert had arranged her travelling documents including five years multiple entry visa with permission to work. He also sent her two thousand pounds with which she obtained a traveller's cheque. Tiana left her job at the health centre in Lagos and her Nigerian friends to meet up with her fiancé in UK with the intention of living happily ever after. She was a university degree holder in social healthcare and Hubert was a college trained carer in UK. Aside from her love life, Tiana's story and life journey hadn't really been a fairy tale.

Chapter Three

A Drop Of Mercy

The empty plot of land by the side of Iperu Waterside Inn constantly gave off pungent smells because of its garbage area which was used as a dumping ground for waste disposal. The introduction of the surrounding vegetation was an attempt to minimise and absorb the stench. The only attraction the inn offered to her guests was the serenity of the River Ogun and her beautiful waterside views. A faint cry was heard by the garbage area. Once again, a silly human had dumped her baby in the bin area, blood was all over her and one could tell that she was just few hours old. Monday, 5th February 1989.

PANSY'S CHEST

The garbage area was becoming a notorious spot for abandoning babies. The general belief was that the prostitutes that hung around the inn slept with the guests, got pregnant, disappeared and later came back to drop their babies by the bin. This was the seventh baby Pansy was picking up from the garbage side. The twenty three year old lady had come to the inn for a business meeting that lasted well into the night. It was about one o'clock in the morning when her driver called her attention to the scream from the bin area.

Pansy was tired. The evil plot had produced yet another baby; seven in total. What was she to do? She couldn't walk away though she had a good mind to do so; after all she was not the Ogun State government. These prostitutes should all be banned from hanging around the inn, Pansy thought. The baby's cries continued. With blood all over her and the placenta and umbilical cord still hanging to her body, Pansy hurriedly picked her up, used her scarf to wrap her gently and headed for the health care unit of Iperu Police Department. She had the intention of leaving her in the health care unit, after reporting the matter and going home.

PANSY'S CHEST

Throughout the fifteen minutes journey, the baby's yells were very loud and deafening. She must have been very hungry and tired. On getting to the healthcare unit, the baby's yells continued as the staff received them. She was registered with the healthcare unit who filed the police report. The staff then took the baby from Pansy and hurriedly cleaned her up, dressed and fed her. They returned to the reception with the baby, all fed and awake.

As Pansy was about to leave, the baby chuckled. There was silence in the room. She had been too tired to look at the baby, besides it was pitch dark when she found her. She didn't care as she was exhausted. However, she turned on instinct to look at the baby in the room for the first time. The baby was a very tiny pretty girl and she smiled with her tearful eyes. She had blonde hair, hazel eyes and very dark skin. Pansy thought that was a very rare combination in this part of the world.

Pansy's heart skipped a bit as she reached out for her tiny palm with her index finger. The baby clenched it and chuckled. The baby's chuckles echoed in her head. She was such a beautiful baby, with unusual body features. With the permission of the relevant authorities, Pansy took the baby to OCHS, where babies were looked after till they were nineteen years old. As was her custom with the other six babies she brought, she proceeded to name and bless the baby. She had been so captivated by the baby's beauty that she exclaimed 'Black Princess'! 'Tiana! Tiana means princess. You have been rescued like the others my black princess; Tiana Noire. Though I am tired, the timing for God's mercies never run out; Ileanuoluwakisu. May the seasons of God's mercies never run out on us. Amen'.

Though she didn't have time to look after children personally, Pansy sponsored the babies by way of financial aid. Tiana was one of the seven babies to benefit from Pansy's kind gesture, apart from the other twenty three children. That was how Tiana started at OCHS before proceeding to the University.

Now Tiana was about to leave the shores of the country for a white man's land, the United Kingdom. On bidding farewell to everyone, Tiana left Murtala Mohammed airport for Gatwick airport on 1st March 2012. She had never been to the airport as she never thought of the day she would be privileged to travel. Even when Hubert chatted with her online, she looked forward to the day he would lose interest in her and leave. The day never came and now she was headed for UK to meet him in person for the first time. He had instructed her to always ask for direction any time she felt confused or lost.

The airport bustled with lots of activities with different people doing different things. When her flight was announced Tiana was so happy that she walked briskly through immigration and the departure hall into the plane. She didn't believe she was entering the plane. She located her seat by the window. The big bird was so massive that she became intimidated and scarred. She thought of changing her mind and getting off. 'This sure didn't feel right', she thought. Suddenly, she didn't want to be on the big bird any more. As she was contemplating what to do next, the air hostess walked gently beside her and nudged her to fasten her seat belt. That was when she saw another hostess in front demonstrating. All these were new to her and she complied, there was no room to argue.

As the plane taxied away, she became nauseated and began to panic. The traveller seating next to her encouraged her to be calm. Then she found herself in the air above the clouds. She felt like a real princess about to conqueror an unknown territory. She smiled at the passenger beside her and he smiled back. She expressed her fears and confided in him that it was her first time in the air. He reassured her that all would be well. Soon meals were served and Tiana ate all that she was offered and watched the movie shown on screen, before finally drifting off to sleep.

It was nearly five o'clock when they arrived at Gatwick airport. As the big bird began her descent, Tiana screamed out loud saying that she wasn't feeling well, the passengers around her tried to calm her down once more. On landing, another air hostess came to her rescue. She tried to contact Hubert but he didn't answer the phone. Next she sent a text message to inform him of her arrival and he replied and instructed her on what to do. She went through immigration successfully having satisfied all the travel requirements. She was very excited, yet nervous. Prior to the day, she had only seen white people from a distance, but now she was seeing them at close range. They were to her like the angels she had read about in books; very impeccable.

She was brought back to consciousness by the harshness of the cold weather. Suddenly she wasn't sure she wanted to go ahead with the plan as she felt very cold. She had a jumper and a jacket on but she still felt very cold. 'Was it too late to turn back'? She looked out of the window at the big bird, it seemed it was now too late too turn back. She must face the unknown future with confidence. She thought to herself 'so this is where everyone called Jand. Tiana has now landed in Jand'! She smiled to herself, braced up and preceded with confidence to the arrival hall.

She didn't see Hubert but she received a text message from him which instructed her to board the train from Gatwick airport to East Croydon Station. Luckily she had one hand luggage and a moderately sized suitcase. 'This country called Jand was so cold', she thought. The trains and tubes were definitely bigger than the trains in Nigeria. While some travelled on the road level, some travelled on the underground and few went in air above the street level. There were lots of people on the train and she soon discovered that she wasn't the only black person around. She saw people of all shades and ethnicity. From East Croydon station, she was then instructed to take a black cab to Croham Park bed and breakfast. She saw lots of trees and greens on the way; there were also woodlands and acres of parkland with mature trees. She saw cattle and sheep grazing pasture. A reservation had been made for her at the bed and breakfast and by the time she checked into the room, she was so tired that she fell asleep.

Chapter Four

A Ray Of Hope

On waking up in the evening, there was still no sign of Hubert. She was hungry and went to get some drink at the bar. There were some cakes and bars of chocolate on sale so she got some to eat too. She observed that she was the only black female and this intimidated her further. By the following day, she went down for breakfast at eight o'clock and made enquiries about feeding arrangements. The concept of a lodge that served only breakfast was quite new to Tiana. She showed them her travel documents and explained that she was a stranded migrant waiting for her fiancé. She never mentioned that it was an online affair that would have been too embarrassing for her.

PANSY'S CHEST

The staff at the bed and breakfast was helpful and sympathetic to her plight. The meal was quite filling and healthy and she met few people. Some were students and others were tourists or workers. When she inquired, they showed her the eateries she could visit in the area, as well as the markets. Tiana proceeded to make alternative arrangements for her other meals.

Everyone tried to be courteous at Croham Park bed and breakfast. There were fights, mostly from the bar section, when few people got drunk so there was constant police patrol at nights around and their job was to maintain sanity and arrest trespassers. Most residents kept to themselves and the few that mingled were very lively. They met at the bar section in the evenings, while some drank and chatted away into the night, others danced. Tiana mingled with the residents at the bar and danced her heart out but always returned to her room depressed. Her heart was very heavy as a result of Hubert's unexplainable absence and silence.

Another virtue she had was that she never got drunk. She had read enough to know that she needed to save money. She refrained from bringing her previous unethical dating habits to the bar and also avoided flirting with men or being tempted to date them. She set her hopes on seeing Hubert and it was important for her to convey a healthy image of a decent lady, should he walk in at anytime.

Days rolled by yet Hubert failed to turn up. There was no further instruction from him nor was there any communication or information about him since she arrived at the bed and breakfast. All the while, she pondered on different thoughts. 'Was Hubert ill? Was he involved in an accident? Was he dead? Did he have a change of mind about the engagement and marriage proposal? Did he sight her afar off, became disinterested and decided to discontinue the relationship? Perhaps it was someone that pulled a trick on her. It was all so good to be true. But why? Who would carry out such an expensive joke? What did they stand to gain from someone like her? Some people must have lied to her'. Tiana didn't want to return to Nigeria, yet she was so let down and broken hearted that she had been strung by a series of lies from a guy she met online. She felt really confused.

A week before her rent ran out, she went to the bar one evening to have a glass of juice. She met an elderly couple in their sixties; George and Rose Freeman. Prior to the evening, whenever she saw them in the bar section she always exchanged pleasantries. On this occasion, she took the conversation further by explaining her dilemma to them. She didn't mention the fact that she had never met Hubert or that it was an online affair. She told them that she had met her fiancé in Nigeria and had been engaged. She then said that they had both agreed to meet in the bed and breakfast in UK but he had walked out on her and she was stranded. She showed the couple her travel documents and they promised to help.

George commented on her look. He was surprised that with her blonde hair and hazel eyes, she was Nigerian. He had seen people with similar features in New Guinea and Papua New Guinea a couple of years back, when he went with some friends on vacation to Africa. Tiana smiled and remained silent. She explained that she grew up in the orphanage and never met her real parents.

What attracted the Freeman couple to Tiana was the fact that she had a university degree in social healthcare and she seemed to have a calm personality. The Freeman couple was getting old and needed a house keeper to help them care for their home and supervise the staff in the garden, which was twenty minutes away. Up until they met Tiana, they both ran their affairs. If Tiana agreed to help out, she would be allowed to work for them from nine o'clock in the morning to six o'clock in the evening. In return, she would receive free accommodation and feeding and six hundred pounds monthly. They also agreed to support her in enrolling for short courses to keep her updated in her social healthcare discipline.

Five years would be enough for her to discover what happened to Hubert. This would inform her decisions on the next line of action, should her fiancé fail to turn up or should he decide to end the engagement. She accepted the job offer and in return the Freeman assisted Tiana in settling down.

The Freeman lived in a cottage in Sanderstead. Next door was another cottage occupied by an elderly couple Dr Fraser and Matron Kathryn Jack. On retirement, they ran a respite home together with their four sons. Their half acre garden was also sectioned with hedges and well landscaped with trees and flowers to aid the healing process. The Jacks had a cat called Eazzie, who loved to come round the Freeman Gardens. She was a regular guest who was always entertained. Eazzie cat was allowed to play in both gardens and visitors to the respite home found him entertaining.

Tiana had to clean the house daily, sort out the laundry, go shopping and handle the Freeman's administrative tasks. The Freeman had two dogs that Tiana had to walk (round the garden) in the morning and evenings. The interesting thing about the couple was their love for pigeons. They ensured that birdfeed and water were available daily to encourage the birds feed in their garden. The birds were fed twice a day; at the start of Tiana's work and when she was closing. Thus the evenings always ended with sound of birds chirping away.

The meals were always prepared by Rose and Tiana assisted when she was less busy. This was Tiana's first experience with a British family. Three of the men she met at Croham Park bed and breakfast were also staff in the Freeman Garden. They tended to the animals, helped with the farming and delivered the farm produce to the market for sale. They also took it in turns to take the unprocessed diary products to the food factory for processing. Apart from the house keeping role, Tiana had to supervise the three staff and ensure they performed their daily duties. She found the job quite amazing but demanding, yet she was determined to make a success of her trip to London. Any job would do for a first timer in UK.

The Freeman couple were a hardworking couple and as she worked with them Tiana understood why they needed help. She hardly knew anywhere except Croham Park bed and breakfast, Sanderstead High Street and the town shops. She barely knew anyone except the Freeman couple and their friends. She hardly saw the Jacks next door although Eazie cat was a constant garden visitor. The neighbourhood was so quiet and different to what she knew in Nigeria.

Many questions flooded her mind as the days progressed. How could Hubert do this to her? Why did he send her all those gifts if he didn't love her? Why did he spend over a year chatting with her if it was all going to fizzle out like this? With time she found herself arguing his absence away. 'If he didn't love her, he won't have given her money or guided her to UK', she heard herself saying intermittently. Or was he insane? Was he a psychopath? Had she fallen for a maniac'? The thought of being asked to return to Nigeria made her refrain from going to the police to investigate, she only hoped for the best. Before the expiration of her permit to stay she hoped Hubert would turn up or a more positive thing would happen, maybe she would find someone else.

Chapter Five

The Devil In The Details

Rose was the first to wake up daily, rising as early as six o'clock. She was passionate about cooking fresh meals daily and watering her indoor plants. She was so obsessed with her kitchen and cooking that she prepared all the meals eaten in the house. That was her sacred place, where she first communed with God and her day. Next she read the newspapers that were dropped through her post at seven o'clock and by nine o'clock when Tiana resumed, Rose would be on the sofa listening to her favourite radio show. On resumption, Tiana set the breakfast table for George.

By September 2012, the Freeman assisted Tiana in enrolling

for short part time courses in Personnel Development and Management in Social Healthcare Systems at Croydon College while she worked in Freeman Home and Garden in between her studies. Though she met a number of people in school, she didn't have enough time to develop well meaning friendships.

On her arrival in the Freeman home initially, she fulfilled the role of a house keeper. By the end of her third year, she satisfied the requirements and was given the role of a home and garden administrator; a position she occupied for the next two years. Tiana learnt more about the family one Saturday afternoon, as they prepared for lunch, during her third year in the Freeman household. Saturday 4th August 2015.

The sixty three year old couple had been married for forty seven years. Both were high school lovers who married at sixteen, despite their families' objections that they were too young. They met at a prom date, took to each other, got married and had two children; a forty three year old lady, Dora Janelle and a forty seven year old son, Tom Jayden. Dora was born with feeding and breathing complications and her disability meant she had to be kept in a care home under specialised relief equipments in Riddlesdown. Proceeds from the Freeman Garden as well as government support were used to maintain the family. George and Rose were farmers. While Rose specialised in animal farming, George was into general farming (mainly crops, fruits and vegetables). Between the two, they had three paid staff.

Tom had grown up with them like an only child and was a very lively but shy boy. He was also a very intelligent boy who loved adventures. At sixteen he joined a group of tourists and by seventeen they had gone round Europe on tour. In his nineteenth year, the tourist group decided to explore Africa. They booked a trip to five African countries; Tunisia, Kenya, Egypt, South Africa and Nigeria, spending two weeks in each. Nigeria was the last port of call, before returning to UK. The group aimed to travel round the world, a step at a time.

According to reports, the tourists had gone to watch a theatre show at a cinema and there had been a bomb explosion, which razed down the entire building, left the surrounding buildings in deplorable states and injured passers-by. There were no survivors from Electra Film House. On hearing the news, the world was shattered as well as the concerned authorities in UK and Nigeria. There was one question on everyone's mind, 'Why was the devil involved in the tourists travelling plans'? The tourist had gone on brilliant outings for over three years and had enjoyed successful tours of Europe in the last two. Their tour of African countries was almost a complete victory too but for the Show Night; the night the devil was included in the details. It was Thursday evening, 2nd. May 1987 and they were scheduled to return to UK that weekend.

At the time of the attack, the UK authorities had reported political instability in the country as a likely motivation for the attack. On hearing the news, the Freeman couple were so devastated. Tom was their only able bodied son and his disabled sister was in a care home. This was before the neighbours next door converted their home to a respite centre. In despair, the Freeman couple turned to each other for comfort. The Jacks were still in active medical service, so they made arrangements for them to get access to qualitative counselling. It had been twenty eight years since the fateful day of the dreadful attack. Healing had taken place but the void left by Tom was irreplaceable.

According to Rose, Tiana reminded them of their son Tom, when she approached them, introduced herself as a Nigerian and said that she was stranded. She imagined how Tom must have felt the moment the bomb exploded and the building went up in flames. Tiana was the only Nigerian lady in Sanderstead, in fact the only black female among the whites. Tiana said that she was sorry to hear about the family's tragic incidence but Rose insisted that it had been part of the healing process, to have talked about it.

It then occurred to Rose that all they had done since the fateful event was to light candles and lay wreathes at the British High Commission, year after year for about ten years. They had met with other European families of the deceased tourists and the pains had been too much for them to bear as bitterness and anger were heard in their voices. With time, they lost contact with these families.

PANSY'S CHEST

While speaking with Tiana, Rose had an idea to visit the scene of their son's death and hold a memorial service with other families of victims of the blast in Nigeria. She wanted to confront the reality of what took place twenty eight years ago. She planned to go to Nigeria, hoping to find out what had actually happened. Rose felt Tiana's coming to UK was timely and requested for her assistance with the investigations in Nigeria. She assured Tiana that if she spent the remaining two years with them, they could all accompany her to Nigeria and help her settle down.

Tiana was quietly disappointed on hearing this. Three years on, she still hoped Hubert would turn up and she won't have to hang around the Freeman couple or return to Nigeria. She had given up her life in Nigeria and hoped that her fate in UK wouldn't end in disaster. Tiana needed a strategy to pull through the phase of having to cope with life's disappointments. Firstly she had left the good job she had at the healthcare centre in Lagos; next Hubert had abandoned her in the bed and breakfast. Then the Freeman couple wanted her to return home on expiration of her work permit and assist them in carrying out an investigation on their son's death as well as join them in his memorial service.

Although she was reluctant to go to Nigeria, she knew she had to prepare for eventualities. Should she have to return to Nigeria in the next two years, she would have to save some money for her trip and initial maintenance in Nigeria. The Freeman couple worshipped at the Parish Church Saint James Riddlesdown and Tiana joined them. The church encouraged her congregation to support the children's church and Tiana was one of the few members that volunteered to teach. She soon realised her love for children and in the next two years, she availed herself and took up short courses in child health care. She believed that if she did return to Nigeria, the knowledge of child health care would boost her employment chances. She would then have the option to work either as an adult healthcare officer or a child healthcare officer.

In response to the Freeman's request for Tiana to help with investigations in Nigeria, Tiana contacted her friends Chioma, Habiba and Ewaoluwa. She believed they could help with the initial investigations. On contacting them, she was too ashamed to confess what had happened to her and her fiancé. She told them that they had both decided to part ways and she would be in Nigeria at the expiration of her five year visa. They hadn't heard from her in three years and the last they heard from her was when she called them from the bed and breakfast to notify them of her arrival in England. Her friends wanted the details so they probed further. She eventually told them what happened. They were sorry to hear her romance tale ended in disappointment.

Chioma and Habiba had completed their National Youth service program outside Lagos and had found good jobs and were working in Lagos. Ewaoluwa was still teaching at her nursery. Tiana also contacted the staff at OCHS for assistance. Two years was enough for them to plan the Freeman's visit to Nigeria. She secretly hoped that Hubert would turn up and she wouldn't have to go with the Freeman couple. There were many questions to be answered. For example, they needed to know the people with Tom and his tourist friends when the blast happened on 2nd May 1987. After twenty eight years, do these people still have families, if so where were their families? What did the families know about the incidence on the fateful night? Where did Tom's European Tour group visit in Nigeria and where did they stay? Based on the findings of the authorities at that time, what was the public's opinion; was it an accidental bombing or a terrorist attack?

According to Chioma's findings, the bomb blast had taken place at the site presently occupied by The Conqueror Cinema. That was where Electra Film House Surulere used to be before it was razed down. The Conqueror Cinema was built there to make a bold statement of tenacity. To further reaffirm the people's hope, a masjid was attached to the left of The Conqueror Cinema and a chapel was attached to the right. These three buildings now occupied the area that was once razed down by the blast. The twenty six year old Chioma worked in Victoria Island, which was far from the scene of the accident so she didn't have the time to visit Surulere for further investigations.

However Habiba worked in Surulere so she volunteered to

visit the chaplain at Mercy Chapel; the chapel attached to the The Conqueror Cinema. Habiba briefed the chaplain on her mission. The sixty seven year old chaplain, Reverend Iyanuloluwa Igbagbo – Durotimi promised to make enquiries for them. After asking around, the chaplain referred Habiba to the former chaplain, Reverend Olurantimi Omoba-Asejere.

Reverend Iyanuloluwa informed Habiba that Reverend Olurantimi was one of the founding fathers of Mercy Chapel, and though he is retired, he still officiates as a minister and had an office within the chaplaincy. He was the best lead the London team could get in the course of their mission to Nigeria. Through the reverend, Habiba was able to get an appointment to see the retired chaplain. She kept the appointment with Reverend Olurantimi and told him of the impending visit by Tiana and her London friends. He listened to the twenty seven year old but said little. He assured her that a memorial service was possible when the London team arrived. Tiana's friends then assured her that that they were able to organise and manage all activities involved with the London team's visit to Nigeria. Wednessday, 4th January 2017.

Chapter Six

The Mission To Africa

The Freeman couple spent the next two years trying to locate other families of the deceased tourists in Europe. Most of those Rose heard about had either died or were too old to respond. However she was able to get in touch with three people who claimed to be relatives of the victims of the 1987 Show Night. They were Sammy Godwin from Cardiff, Tricia Warren from Eastbourne and Zelda Topping from Derbyshire. The five Britons including George and Rose Freeman decided to travel down to Nigeria and hold a memorial service to mark the thirtieth anniversary of the Shownight at Mercy Chapel. These formed the London Team and Tiana was assigned to lead the delegate.

PANSY'S CHEST

To commemorate the occasion, they arranged with a tourist company to visit the five African countries; Tunisia, Kenya, Egypt, South Africa and Nigeria, spending two weeks in each. The six left for the ten week tour on 21st February 2017 and arrived in Nigeria on the 18th April 2017.

Tiana's friends met the London Team at Murtala Mohammed airport and a hired mini bus took them all to a five star hotel; Glorious Hotel and Suites in Surulere, which was ten minutes walk to Mercy Chapel. It was the same hotel Tom and his friends had checked into thirty years back. It was the state of the art hotel and the choice of hotel was based on its proximity to the National Stadium and the National Arts Theatre. The stadium had hosted the international football tournament in the previous year and the National Arts Theatre had hosted the world to a festival of arts and culture.

The London team checked into the hotel before making their way to see the retired chaplain at seven o'clock in the evening. They had just finished a communion service at Mercy Chapel and retired seventy four year old Reverend Olurantimi welcomed his guests. They all went to the chapel's cafe for dinner. Although short and robust, he was a learned gentleman and had good command of the English language. He had trained in a seminary in northern Nigeria and had served as a priest in different parts of the country, before being posted to Mercy Chapel. He was also a very bubbly man who made every effort to make the evening interesting.

The London team told him that they planned to spend two weeks in Nigeria; recapturing the final moments of their deceased. They would end the tour with a memorial service on the exact day of the blast, 2nd May 2017 and return to London by the weekend. Reverend Olurantimi asked the London team to see him the next day. He asked Tiana to excuse the London Team the next day, as he preferred to speak with them privately. He suggested she went out with her friends for a reunion and join them later in the evening.

On the second day of their arrival in Nigeria, Tiana met up with her friends at the chapel's cafe. There were lots of laughter and tears as they spoke about their experiences since they all left school. Chioma worked in a bank, Ewaoluwa was still running her school, Ewa Singh-Raj Nursery School. Habiba also ran her own business; a restaurant. They said that they were sorry that Tiana had been betrayed by love and caught up in the Freeman's affairs. Their tales of romance didn't sound exciting or successful either.

Habiba and Chioma gave up on online dating after hearing that Hubert had varnished at the bed and breakfast. They made nice friends online but they had no serious commitments. Prior to Tiana's arrival, they had just supported Ewaoluwa in getting back up after a traumatic past. It had been five years since Tiana left the shores of Nigeria and her friends had been working hard in their fields to gain economic empowerment and financial freedom. Chioma also had dreams of taking a masters program in Birmingham and had saved towards it.

Before her arrival, Tiana had got in touch with the healthcare centre she worked with in Lagos. They were glad to hear from her but didn't have any vacancy. She had also sent her curriculum vitae to health sectors across the country to see if she could work with her freshly acquired skills but she got no response. Tiana gave her curriculum vitae to the chaplain too. He promised to put her forward for job offers once the memorial service was over and the rest of the London Team was back in London.

Meanwhile during the meeting with the London Team, Reverend Olurantimi apologised to the five guests for excluding Tiana. He felt they had come on a sacred mission that was sensitive and private. Being one of the founding fathers of Mercy Chapel, he knew a lot about the chapel as well as the incidents that surrounded its formation. He also had significant information about the Show Night and would share this with them; offering some counselling where necessary.

He was reliably informed that on the said date, the foreign nationals were on holidays in Nigeria and went with a group to watch a theatre performance in Electra Film House. There had been a bomb blast, the cinema building had been razed down and the surrounding buildings were badly damaged. There were no survivors in the cinema building. Glorious Hotel and Suites Surulere reported that four British nationals, three European nationals, and seven Africans (including three Nigerians) had checked in as tourists. The fourteen youths were aged between eighteen and twenty five years old. They were due to check out at the weekend. The last time they were seen at the hotel was on Thursday morning.

The city had been traumatised on Thursday night, locally known as 'Show Night'. By Friday morning, when the tourist didn't turn up for breakfast, the hotel authorities were alarmed, 'fourteen youths was a large number to miss'! By Saturday morning there was no sign of the tourists and the hotel authorities had to alert the organisation responsible for the tourists in Nigeria. By Sunday morning when the group was meant to check out, there was no trace of them, only their possessions were in the hotel rooms. It was discovered that the youths were scheduled to attend the show at the cinema on the Show Night. Investigations gathered from close sources confirmed that the youths were seen entering the building minutes prior to the blast. That was the last account. The assumption was that they all went in for the theatre show.

After giving the account on his findings, the retired chaplain encouraged his guests to stay on for the evening service at Mercy Chapel before retreating to their rooms. He requested that the London team see him on day three and Tiana would hang out with her friends again. The retired chaplain had made some enquiries and discovered few members of the families of the victims of the Show night in Nigeria.

On their third day in Lagos, the London Team met with three elderly Nigerians who were relatives of the victims of the Show Night. The Oluwaloju and Ireadale families were next door neighbours. Oluwafemifunre and Motolawo Oluwaloju were Claudia's parents while Eunice Ireadale was Sandra's mum, her father was late. Both Claudia and Sandra were caught in the blast. As far as these elderly Nigerians were concerned, their children were in school studying on the Show Night. These girls were later reported missing by their room mates and class mates when they failed to turn up in their respective rooms and classes in the week following the Show

PANSY'S CHEST

Night.

The twenty three years old neighbours Claudia and Sandra both attended Yaba college of Technology Lagos. Sandra studied fashion design and Claudia studied theatre arts. Both lives had been cut short, like candles in the wind. According to eighty years old Oluwafemifunre, the political tension between the civilians and the military government may have led to the unfortunate incidence. The once favoured centre for youths and film lovers had become a haven of torment.

'Oh God, why was the cinema built in the first place? Why did the devil choose to come to Surulere? Why did the terrorists strike? What was going on in the terrorists minds? Did the terrorists not have loving parents, adorable kids or faithful friends? Perhaps no one prayed for them on the day of their birth', lamented seventy five years old Motolawo, as she burst into tears. Oluwafemifunre wept along with his wife. The pains could still be heard in their voices thirty years later.

'Claudia loved the cinema and always thought of the day

when she would be a renowned actress. Perhaps she would feature in local, national and international movies someday. She was well behaved and that act of going to the cinema when she was meant to be in school was her first juvenile act', recounted Motolawo, as she sobbed loudly.

Sandra's mother; fifty three year old Eunice joined in the wailing, 'my God my God. Sandra was Claudia's best friend. Sandra had vowed to be responsible for all Claudia's costumes, when she became a movie star. Sandra would be a fashion model, an international icon. Now all their hopes went up in flames as their ashes went down with the blast'. The London team burst into tears too.

Reverend Olurantimi had to intervene as the room gradually turned to a wailing haven. Eight elderly people wailing in his office! He was forced to halt the session to give a little exaltation and motivational sermon. When the situation was under control, he ordered for some tea and biscuits for his guests. He prayed for them and they left.

Chapter Seven

A Stroke Of Luck

On day four, the eight elderly people turned up at the chaplaincy again for more briefing on the program lined up. The emotions were very high and sad like the previous day so the retired chaplain proceeded to encourage them further with his own testimony. Reverend Olurantimi told them that he had lost his seventeen year old ward, in the blaze too. The room went silent. George asked him why he had been silent on his loss for so long. The retired chaplain said that it was his responsibility to deal with his hurts privately, so it didn't affect those he should be ministering to.

PANSY'S CHEST

Reverend Olurantimi's seventeen years old ward, Effiong Abasiama had lived with him while his daughter Pansy, shuttled between his Lagos residence and her mother's house in Ibadan. The reverend heard that Pansy had been a loving lady but a rebellious party animal. She was meant to accompany Effiong to Electra Film House but couldn't because she had promised her mother to see her in Ibadan the next morning. Pansy dropped Effiong at the cinema in the evening and later went off to Ibadan. That was her narrow escape on the 1987 Show Night.

While residing in Ibadan in 1964, Reverend Olurantimi met a lady at a wedding where he was the best man and she was the chief bride's maid. She was Lady Morewa Adunni Fisher, a very beautiful and wealthy politician. At the evening party, the twenty one year old Olurantimi (not yet a priest then), got carried away with Lady Mo's charisma and ended up having a one night stand with her. He communicated with Lady Mo daily for several weeks and promised to marry her. When she informed him that she was pregnant, he got scarred. A pauper like him couldn't afford a lady like her then, nor the pregnancy. He wanted to go to the seminary and having a child outside wedlock was not part of the plan. He reasoned that Lady Mo wouldn't fit in well as a preacher's wife so he distanced himself from her.

Sad and dejected, the twenty year old Lady Mo wept bitterly. The implication was that she had to raise her child alone in her Ibadan mansion built for her by her father, Otunba Charles Ayiludun Fisher; a prominent politician and philanthropist in Ibadan then.

Determined to give her child the best, Lady Mo decided to sponsor Olurantimi to the seminary. He eventually graduated and agreed to allow his teenage daughter, Pansy Omoba– Asejere spend some of her holidays with him at his various priestly posts. Reverend Olurantimi got transferred to a diocese in Ogun state in 1983 while Pansy was a student at Ogun State University. She changed her name from Pansy Omoba - Asejere to Pancy Jere Fisher. All Pansy's lectures were from Mondays to mid day on Thursdays, so her affluent political mum encouraged her to spend Thursdays to Sundays with her in her Ibadan mansion.

Lady Mo hosted politicians in her home daily so meals were prepared in the Fisher Empire daily; it was like a party scene. Lots of political meetings and rallies also took place within the Fisher Empire. Pansy was given her own wing within the empire where provision was made for her and her guests.

Reverend Olurantimi insisted Pansy spent her lecture days with him in the vicarage at Ogun State University. This was to ensure he kept an eye on her when she was in Ogun State University. Her parents didn't want her in the hostel because of her wild character. Pansy later finished her political science degree at the university in 1987 and joined her mother in politics. When the reverend got transferred to Mercy Chapel, he insisted that Pansy continued to spend the same amount of time with him in Lagos, as she did while in the university. He felt that it would be good for her political career too. Pansy was thrilled; it meant she could reach more people in Lagos through her father. This motivated Lady Mo to get the reverend his own accommodation in Lagos.

PANSY'S CHEST

Periodically members of the congregation requiring accommodation stayed with Pansy and her father; Effiong Abasiama was one of them. The reverend met her parents in Cross river state where he had been on a mission. On hearing that he was based in Lagos, they asked him to accommodate Effiong. She was an education student at the Teacher's Training College Yaba but having challenges with securing accommodation.

Chapter Eight

Echoes Of The Past

Reverend Olurantimi continued his narration of what he heard from close sources. He was informed that shortly after she left school and joined her mother in politics; Pansy discovered that her mother was critically ill. In an effort to remain in control, she had turned to a lifestyle of drugs and alcohol. Unfortunately he wasn't aware of the development because he never noticed any unusual behaviour in her when she came to visit him in Lagos. Her last visit to him was when she took Effiong to the cinema. It was assumed then that she couldn't handle Effiong's death and her mother's illness. That was the message she communicated to him, whenever he called her to ask her why she stopped visiting.

PANSY'S CHEST

It was further reported that few weeks after the 1987 Show Night, lady Mo passed away at the age of forty three and Pansy was further devastated. She refused to go to Lagos but preferred to perform her mourning rites in Ibadan. Reverend Olurantimi sent his condolence to her but all efforts to convince her to go to Lagos proved abortive. Her mother had willed the mansion in Ibadan to her and though Pansy loved her father, she hated living in his house in Lagos. The lifestyle of the priest was very different to a politician's lifestyle. She gradually distanced herself from her father in Lagos and chose to live in Fisher Empire Ibadan.

The reverend was told that as Pansy continued in her lifestyle of drugs and alcohol, the political integrity and image of Fisher Empire dwindled; the politicians acknowledged that a Jezebel had taken over and soon stopped visiting the Empire. Within two years, Pansy's destructive habits eventually led to a deterioration of her health. Fisher Empire was converted to a rehabilitation centre when Pansy was diagnosed with lung cancer and kidney challenges at the age of twenty four. Pansy's Chest became her rehabilitation chest.

PANSY'S CHEST

While in the university, Pansy got involved with different philanthropic exercises and charities and she continued with them till she passed away at the age of forty three. Upon her death, she left Pansy's Chest in the care of her partners. At this point, Reverend Olurantimi wiped the tears off his eyes and the room was thrown into silence. It was the guests' turn to comfort the reverend.

It was about six o'clock in the evening when Tiana joined the reverend and the rest of the London team to discuss their plans for the coming days. Rose informed the team of her findings from the travel agency used by Tom and his friends. They had given her the program of events for the 1987 tour. The London Team planned to be prayerfully engaged with similar activities to mark their families' final moments on earth before the blast. They believed that it was a way to feel what they would have felt back then and a way to pray genuinely for the repose of their souls and thank God for their lives. Tiana's friends in turn planned the program of events for 2017 tour.

PANSY'S CHEST

Firstly they booked some tickets to watch a national match at the national stadium on day five and they bought some tickets to watch the local drama at the National Arts Theatre on day six. Claudia's parents Motolawo and Olufemifunre chose to opt out of these two events but promised to join them on their visit to the local markets in Yaba and Surulere on the seventh day. Sandra's mum Eunice agreed to participate in all the events.

The Ireadale and Oluwaloju families volunteered to join the London team on their visit to the bomb site on the eight day. They would all stop for an evening meal like the tourists did thirty years earlier and attend the theatre dance at The Conqueror Cinema afterwards. A silent prayer would be said after the dance in memory of the youths that never made it back to their hotel rooms. The memorial service would be held on the ninth day at Mercy Chapel to be attended by the families of the victims.

According to the travel agency, the tourists were scheduled for the beach the day after seeing the show, so all the families agreed to go to the Eleguishi Royal Beach in Leki the day after the memorial service. Going to the beach would be their final outing before heading back to their destination in UK. Unlike the tourists that planned to go for leisure in 1987, their family members would be there for a Christian retreat in 2017. Everyone agreed to the plan and decided that the remaining three days would be left open for the London team to relax and explore Nigeria.

On their way back to the hotel, George began to reflect on all he had just heard. No wonder the reverend was really sympathetic to the London Team and his Nigerian guests. He had also been affected; losing a ward and his daughter narrowly escaping the blast. He had briefed them with such precision and accuracy. Tiana interrupted his flow of thoughts and invited the London team to OCHS and Pansy's Chest Ibadan. She told them that she wanted to visit the two places.

She entertained them with stories of how she had grown up in the home, the sort of things they did and the pranks they played. She also told them of how she was particularly grateful when they were finally allowed out of OCHS at week ends and how much impact the home had on her. The London team agreed that it was a good idea but advised that the visits be scheduled until after the memorial service.

On day nine, the memorial service was held at Mercy Chapel, where the theme was on the need to forgive and how everyone needed to ask God for forgiveness too. Reverend Iyanuloluwa ministered healing to them through the word of God, it was a communion service. A reception was organised at the banquet hall of the Glorious Hotel and Suites afterwards. In his characteristic jovial manner, Reverend Olurantimi encouraged all who attended. Although the event marked was a sad one, all who attended received healing and agreed it was a good way to honour their deceased. The only tasks left for the London Team were to accompany Tiana to OCHS on day eleven and Pansy's Chest on day twelve. Sammy Godwin, Tricia Warren and Zelda Topping felt both visits were somewhat private and decided to stay behind in Lagos.

Chapter Nine

From Empire To Chest

Mother Pauline had been informed of the London Team's arrival prior to the day of the visitation. Tiana's friends had helped with the arrangement, though they remained in Lagos. The only reason Mother Pauline remembered Tiana was because of her unique features, that is the blonde hair, unusually dark skin and hazel eyes. She was the only baby that fitted that description in the home. Tiana introduced the Freeman couple as her friends who were visiting Nigeria on a mission. The matron of OCHS, Mother Pauline was presented with flowers and the staff and children were presented with food items, clothes and accessories.

PANSY'S CHEST

Mother Pauline had been in charge of the home before Tiana was brought in as a baby. Now Tiana was twenty eight and she was in her mid sixties, almost retiring. At the time Tiana was brought in, Mother Pauline ran the home with her late husband. The charity was birth when the couple discovered they couldn't have children. Mother Pauline had a trying time with her family and her in-laws as she wept for about eighteen years due to the inhumane way she was treated as a barren woman in Nigeria. The couple later decided to open their home to babies without families to care for them. The home grew gradually and they were able to accommodate children from ages zero to nineteen years.

With government support, they were able to lease one acre of land to accommodate a hundred and twenty children. Through the various programmes they ran in the home and government support, they were also able to fund the settlement package for each child that left the home at nineteen. In the course of running the home, Mother Pauline discovered that the children brought as much joy to them, like any of their own biological children would have brought.

PANSY'S CHEST

Hence the name Oluremilekun meaning God consoled me (wiped my tears).

Mother Pauline also remembered Pansy Jere Fisher; the political philanthropist that brought Tiana. She gave her the name Tiana Noire Ileanuoluwakisu. George then asked for the meaning of Tiana's name. Mother Pauline explained that Pansy told them in OCHS that she was going to overlook Tiana by the bin but she heard a cry for mercy, picked up the baby and took her to health care unit. Next she was going to leave her in the care of the health officials but the tired and worn out Pansy remembered that God's mercies are available at all times of the day and in all seasons. This was what the inspiration behind the name Ileanuoluwakishu; which means that there's no sunset with God's mercy. Her dark skin, blonde hair and hazel eyes were a sensation too. Her looks and her calmness won Pansy's heart as well as the heart of the staff at the home. To Pansy, she was a black princess, hence the name Tiana Noire.

She was the seventh abandoned baby that Pansy brought into

the home. Although she didn't have time to look after the children herself, Pansy sponsored them from the home by providing enough money to meet each child's basic requirements. She also organised with the home that gifts be given to each child on her assumed birthday (the day they were brought into the home). Such were the random acts of love that Pansy rendered and that was still the practise at the OCHS. This had been possible through the generosity of people like Tiana who had passed through their gates and came back to sponsor other children.

Mother Pauline further stated that it was sad that Pansy wasn't there to see Tiana and the other children who had been recipients of her wonderful gestures. The other six children brought into the home by Pansy had each become a success in their fields. There was a teacher, a banker, a professional hair stylist and make up artist, a fashion designer, a drawing artist with own artist studio and the last one had her own catering business. She was glad Tiana was a graduate in health care sector. In response, Tiana made a pledge to give a monthly token of ten thousand naira to OCHS through direct debit and hoped to give more as she settled down in Nigeria.

Mother Pauline then took the team round the home. The children had been prepared for the guest visitors. She introduced Tiana as one of their children who had become very successful and though not prepared, Tiana gave an impromptu speech. She told the children how excited she had been to see the staff and children. She pointed out that though she had been found in the garbage bin at Sagamu, she didn't allow that image to hinder her passion for excellence.

She also told the children that the seven of them that fell into the category of being picked up by the bin since the home began were all successful in their endeavours. She commented on the fact that most of the children were brought in by their parents or relatives, so she expected them to strive for excellence too. It was a moving afternoon. The London team thanked Mother Pauline and the staff at the home and left in the mini bus, which headed for Lagos.

On their way back to Lagos, Tiana remembered her days at

PANSY'S CHEST

OCHS. The place had changed since she left. She wondered what had become of her teenage crushes. Kolapo Andrews, Dandy Omojuola and Patrick Chike. Most of all she was still coming to terms with what had happened between her and Hubert Knight. The bus arrived at Mercy Chapel, where they met the other team members and Reverend Olurantimi, before returning to their rooms at the Glorious Hotel and Suites.

The following day, the Freeman couple and Tiana went to Pansy's Chest in the mini bus. It was a quiet journey and memories of her childhood flooded her mind. Was she really a success like Mother Pauline had told the children in the home? Maybe she just said it to encourage them all or maybe she said it because she saw that George and Rose Freeman were whites. No one explained anything to Mother Pauline or the staff. Tiana had just wasted five years in UK in quest of a lover that never was. She now hoped that she could work and succeed like her friends in Nigeria. The mini bus eventually pulled up at Pansy's Chest about ninety minutes later. Tiana and the London team had never seen such building aesthetics. Pansy's Chest depicted wealth and glamour from the gate to the structures within.

At the gate they were handed an electronic tour guide, which was given to each visitor to help them navigate round the estate. The magnificent gate house was erected beside the gold plaited gate which opened to the one hundred meters drive way; sandwiched between the elongated private gardens used for political rallies. This drive way opened up to an oval road with major axis of about one hundred meters, encircling the one acre Edwardian mansion. The six meters wide oval road had four separate outlets leading to four clusters of three duplexes each.

The first cluster was the recreation cluster, the second was the service cluster, the third was the therapy cluster and the fourth was Pansy's cluster. The recreation cluster consists of a gym and fitness centre and a rest room with a covered terrace leading to the swimming pool. Apart from the recreation cluster which enclosed the swimming pool, the other clusters enclosed the parking lots. The duplexes in each cluster were inter linked by interlocking footpaths with covered walkways leading to the one acre Edwardian mansion. The mansion comprised of twenty room duplex with a pent house. The estate was walled in by beautifully crafted stone wall finish lined with paved stones interspersed with well trimmed hedges. The compound was well landscaped and looked beautiful.

Chapter Ten

An Iota Of Doubt

On alighting from the mini bus, they were directed to the one acre Edwardian mansion. At the entrance to the mansion was a brief history of the Chest, dating back to Lady Morewa's father, Otunba Charles Ayiludun Fisher. He had laid the foundation for the empire but later handed the keys to his daughter on completion of the building structures. The concept behind the empire was Radburn Concept using Radial Clusters. Lady Mo had occupied the mansion while the other functions surrounded her.

Upon Lady Mo's demise, the upper floor and pent house had been occupied by Pansy and her partner, Ronald Bells. The ground floor of the mansion was used as a museum to remember Lady Mo and her father. The administrative office for the Chest was also on the ground floor. When Pansy fell ill, the pent house was reserved for Pansy and Ronald Bells while the upper floor was converted to a hospital to manage her health. The museum on the ground floor was retained. Pansy's cluster was kept for her guests in her life time but when she fell ill, it was used as medical practitioner's cluster, where the team managing her health lived. Upon her death, Pansy's personal effects were also moved into the museum to celebrate the three generation of politicians who had also been philanthropists.

Ronald Bells retained the use of the pent house and the hospital opened up to the public. Private patients who were referred were admitted there and treated accordingly. The service cluster was retained as a maintenance quaters to house all service men and women that served the estate. The therapy cluster was retained for members of the public that were referred to the chest for rehabilitation. It also contained facilities needed for re-integration back into the society. The recreation cluster was converted to a mini club for staff at Pansy's Chest and members of the elite group that could afford to pay. The proceeds from the hospital and museum, therapy and recreation clusters were used to maintain the running of the Chest.

The London team made their way into the reception of the Edwardian mansion where they met the medical director of Pansy's Chest; Dr Praise Olufigbayemi who gave them a warm welcome. He led them into his office. Tiana introduced herself and the London team and thanked Dr Praise for allowing her visit her benefactor's home. They presented the staff with flowers and medical supplies, as requested by Pansy's Chest, when Tiana's friends made enquiries on their needs.

The doctor introduced himself as a fifty six year old trained psychotherapist with good managerial skills. He was often referred to as Doc. He was brought in to oversee the management of Pansy's health from rehabilitation from alcohol and drugs, to stabilisation and death. He was referred to Pansy by one of the politicians that lived near, a very good friend of Lady Mo.

George marvelled at the sound of his name and asked the doctor for the meaning. According to George, it seemed all Nigerian names were tongue twisting sentences. The doctor explained that it was the norm for Nigerians to name their children based on the circumstances surrounding their birth. The doctor proudly claimed that he came from a generation of smart kids. They were always the youngest and smartest in their respective classes. They had a covenant of early success with God who ensured they surpassed their peers in academics and work. The name meant God honoured them before their due season. The Freeman couple were very impressed while Tiana got depressed quietly; she had just lost five years in UK.

Dr O'Figbayemi informed them that as Pansy was losing strength and life was gradually seeping away from her, she appointed trustees to oversee the running of the chest. On appointment, he moved into the medical practitioners' cluster with his medical team. He ran the Chest with two others; Ronald Bells who was the administrator and also Pansy's live in partner, and Donald Porter, who was the occupational therapist; both were European nationals.

He informed them that as part of the initiative to maintain the chest, they encouraged the visitors to go on a guided tour round the estate at the cost of one thousand naira daily. They were also encouraged to pay five hundred naira for the electronic tour guide by the gate. The tours were a form of recreation to those who needed to unwind or be alone. They also provided the opportunity for guests to wait for patients undergoing treatments within the facility.

The doctor said that when he learnt that the London team was coming with Tiana, he volunteered to take them on tour round the Chest. This was their way of welcoming every child they sponsored, who in turn had made a success of her life. Hence it was the tradition in the Chest for one appointed trustee to welcome them. He took them round the museum and the hospital. After about forty five minutes, he led them out of the Edwardian mansion.

As they approached the recreation cluster, Rose asked for the rest room and Dr O'Figbayemi showed her. Suddenly the door to the gym opened and a male voice shouted 'mum'! All eyes turned towards the door as silence filled the air for few minutes. Doc thought to himself 'Who did Ron call mum? Had Ron finally lost it'? He had been talking about returning to UK, but there was a procedure for that and feigning insanity wasn't it.

Doc encouraged the team to seat under the covered terrace as they waited for Rose to use the rest room. He then proceeded to introduce Ronald Bells; the forty nine year old manager and administrator overseeing the running of Pansy's Chest. Ron was Pansy's live in partner, her drug and alcohol habit made it difficult for Ron to propose to her. He had stood beside her as a good friend in their twenty one years together and had loved her so dearly. When they met and fell in love, he had hoped to get married and someday retire to UK with her; leaving the children in Fisher Empire. However, the opportunity never came for marriage or children. They had remained best friends. Rose quickly made her way to the rest room.

Dad! Cried Ron again. George fainted and Tiana caught him just before he fell to the ground. The first aid workers came over to resuscitate him. There was silence again and this was broken by Ron when he exclaimed loudly 'Messy! Messy! Messy! This is really messy'! Doc came to the rescue. 'Ron, this is a team from London. This lady, Tiana is one of the beneficiaries of Pansy's Chest. Pansy sponsored her in OCHS.

Ron further shouted 'Gross! I am done. Perfect. Good job done Doc. I am out of here'. The doctor saw that Don was showing signs of distress, so he calmed him down by offering him a seat and a glass of water. Doc then said 'What exactly is the problem Ron? What is the matter with you? Would you like us to talk about this later in private, after our guests have gone'?

Another white man came to meet them at the covered terrace.

PANSY'S CHEST

'Ron, your attention is needed at the rehab clinic …. Oh dear doc. What's the matter with Don? Is he ill'? The doctor went ahead to introduce the London team to Donald; popularly known as Don. He told them that on Pansy's request the Chest opened up to the public. Addicts in need of reform were brought in, treated and guided back into the society and forty eight year old Donald Porter was the occupational therapist employed to assist. The three men had held forth at Pansy's Chest since her demise.

When Ron regained his composure, he told the doctor that George and Rose Freeman were his parents. George remained silent, steering into the swimming pool. He had just completed the memorial service for his son, Tom Freeman and he didn't want to go insane. Maybe this was how the doctor got his patients. He triggered visitors that came to Pansy's Chest. George was certain that he didn't need counselling or triggering. He continued to stare at the beautiful landscape and pool and chose to remain silent. Rose wasn't back from the rest room so he had to keep calm. Tiana walked over to George to pat his shoulder.

PANSY'S CHEST

She explained to Ron that the Freeman couple had just finished the memorial rites for their son, and were due to be back in UK soon. She had invited them to accompany her to the Chest to see her benefactor's home. She had also heard that it was a master piece opened for public viewing. Ron kept quiet, sat down and starred at the swimming pool too.

Doc got confused and couldn't control himself. 'Ron, are you satisfied now? You sure do need a break'. There was further silence. Tiana was agitated at Ron. Don stepped in. He disclosed the fact that Ron came to Nigeria about thirty years earlier, as Tom Freeman. George passed away in his chair and had to be resuscitated the second time. Luckily this time around, he was seated so he didn't fall. On coming round, he began to yell 'I am a sane man. I still have my sanity. I may be old. It's still intact. I got it all together boys. Tiana, I have to excuse myself, I would not be insulted'. He got up, stormed out of the covered terrace and began to make way to the mini bus in the nearby car park. Ron walked quietly behind him.

Chapter Eleven

Abduction

Don shed more light on Ron as Tiana remained agitated at his behaviour towards George. Don explained that Ron had come with his girlfriend and other tourists to Nigeria thirty years earlier. According to Tom, he said that he went with his friends to watch a theatre show at Electra Film House. The show was to be aired at eight o'clock in the night but at quarter to eight, while they were all seated in the cinema, Ron felt the urge to use the rest room. On his way back, he ran into the most beautiful lady he had ever seen. He found her looks; carriage and charisma were very empowering and decided to stop for a little chat with her.

PANSY'S CHEST

'Hi, I am Tom, Tom Freeman. Here for the theatre too'? The lady replied 'No. I came to drop a friend. I am Pansy Jere-Fisher, enjoy your show'. Tom said that he froze, he had found her voice was very enchanting. 'That was the epitome of grace and beauty', he told Don. He kept staring at the paragon of beauty from her hair to her toe. According to him, she was an African Queen and starring at her made up for the theatre. 'Alright Tom, hurry along and enjoy your show'. He heard Pansy say again.

According to Ron's version of the story, he insisted that they had a glass of wine each but they both ended up having few pints. The next thing he knew, he woke up the following morning in Pansy's Chest; formerly known as Fisher's Empire. He was confused. He felt he had been drugged the night before because he woke up with head ache and was suffering from fainting spells. The door to the place he laid opened and the lady he met in the cinema brought him breakfast in bed. She went ahead and told him about the bomb blast that took place the previous night. Ron said Pansy claimed that they both went for a walk along the streets after having a couple of drinks and getting drunk. Her chauffer located them and assisted them in getting into the car, which was few blocks from the cinema. As they got in, he heard a loud blast, there was chaos and he quickly sped away to safety. The blast happened in Lagos but they found themselves in Ibadan.

Ron later confided in Don that he didn't believe her story initially. 'Why was Pansy not ill in bed too if they were both drunk the night before? That was quite convenient of her to know all the facts; from a drink in the bar in Lagos to her mother's empire in Ibadan'. He bet it was a case of midnight abduction. Pansy then switched on the TV. The media was filled with the news of the horrible blast! The Show Night! Nigeria was in dismay as the world mourned the youths that were caught up in the blast.

Ron's tourist group had been caught up in the blast and he had lost his girlfriend, Tammie Dallas. Ron was gutted and wept for many days. Pansy was by his side to comfort him. Pansy had also lost Effiong, her father's ward whom she took to the cinema. Lady Mo comforted them, though she was very ill at that time. She told Ron that her family and friends would take care of him till he was fit to return to the UK. They also assured him that they would inform the UK and Nigerian authorities too. Ron was housed in one of the flats in Pansy's cluster.

On a monthly basis, a cow was being slaughtered and food was prepared for every one in the empire. The twenty two year old Pansy hosted her friends to food, drinks and drugs. Tom recalled that at nineteen, it was like the best thing that happened to him. He initially hated the drugs, but the glamour was too overpowering. He vowed to control himself. With Pansy, he had it all as luxury and glamour characterised their youth. They were treated like royalty within the empire and were the centre of attraction wherever they went out in a convoy, surrounded by guards. His ethnicity and colour made people worship them, he thought. He was so young and naïve then.

The daily routine for Pansy and Tom was to go to the gym before breakfast. Next they attended to political matters and hosted meetings and rallies in the private gardens just before the gate. They had lunch in the afternoons, went for garden walks and watched films. In the evenings, they had dinner, drank, danced and had themed parties with friends. These included pool, sex, beer and slumber parties etc. With this lifestyle, Ron soon got over his late girlfriend Tammie and his fellow tourists that came from Europe who had died in the blast. There was a lot of money to splash around.

By the time he was mentally fit enough to go out of the empire, he was advised by politicians to change his identity. He had to forget his past, heal and make enough money to go back to UK. Somehow he felt things weren't adding up, but he wanted the life style. If he got tired, he could always return to UK. He had to get as much wealth as he could to resettle in UK with Pansy. He had seen politicians walk into the empire with large bags of foreign currencies. They always talked about businesses, but no one let him in on any. Part of what they wanted him to do was to be an under cover spy, to investigate on the facts of the bombing at the cinema. The politicians had their suspicions and Tom was going to try and get information for the politicians.

With the help of Pansy's mum and her political colleagues, Tom Freeman's identity was changed to Ronald Bells. He was also assigned bodyguards and his own chauffer. He did carry out some private investigations but he got no intelligent leads. About four months after Ron moved in with them, Lady Mo passed away. She died of heart attack, resulting from the chronic chest infections she had experienced for a while. Pansy was totally devastated at Lady Mo's death and Ron was there to console her just as she had been beside him to comfort him at the death of Tammie and the other tourists.

Ron hoped to return to UK with Pansy and wed but there was so much going on for them. With Lady Mo gone, Ron thought he would have more access to the politicians that brought in the bags of money. Rich black fat men and ladies of timber and calibre, some couldn't even speak English. The stage was set for good food, great wine, awesome sex, lively parties and interesting politicians. Time went by quickly and almost two years after they first met, it was discovered that Pansy had severe liver and kidney problems. This was when Ron and Pansy knew the game was over. They had to give up their lifestyle. Her failing health was the motivation for rebranding Fisher Empire and turning it to Pansy's Chest. Pansy lived for another nineteen years while Ron stood by her side.

While Don was speaking with Tiana, George and Rose walked towards them, with Ron following behind. There was anxiety in the atmosphere; it was quite an emotional experience. Tom had explained himself to his parents in the car park, while Don gave Tiana a brief introduction on Ronald Bells. It was an afternoon filled with mixed feelings. Tiana thanked the team at Pansy's Chest and returned to Lagos with George and Rose.

The London team thanked the clergy at Mercy Chapel for the warm reception on their final day in Nigeria. Afterwards, Tiana and her friends went with them to Murtala Mohammed airport; where they boarded the flight back to UK.

Chapter Twelve

The Split

Tiana went to see the chaplain, Reverend Iyanuloluwa on the Monday after the London team left. She took her CV with her because he had promised to put her forward for job vacancies. On arrival at the chaplaincy, the reverend invited her in and asked her to take a seat. He said he would give her the details of who to see for job opportunities. Before then he wanted her to meet the new partners of Mercy Chapel. He told her that Pansy's Chest had signed up with Mercy Chapel so the clergy could minister there and strengthen the religious beliefs of their patients. Monday 1st May, 2017.

PANSY'S CHEST

As he spoke, Ronald Bells walked in with Donald Porter. Tiana was pleased with their arrangements though she wondered why they felt they had to inform her. Initially she thought Pansy's Chest had need for a health officer, so she composed herself. She had previously applied to Pansy's Chest and OCHS and both places said that they didn't have any vacancy. Just as a phone call came in for Don, he left the room. The reverend also excused himself to go to the restroom.

Ron was left alone with Tiana and they both exchanged pleasantries. That was the very first time he would speak to her alone since they met. 'Hello Tiana, I am Tom Jayden Freeman but people know me as Ronald Bells or Ron. Now that was the old me. Please call me Jayden, I am retiring to UK and need a clean start'. Tiana still wondered what the connection was but said 'Hello Sir, I am Tiana, Tiana Noire - Ileanuoluwakisu'. She said that she was pleased Tom Freeman was alive, even though they had held a memorial service for him earlier at Mercy Chapel. She was also grateful that Pansy's Chest had sponsored her at OCHS.

PANSY'S CHEST

'Please call me Jayden. You are a new kid on the block. When I hear Ron, I know it's someone from Pansy's Chest and when I hear Tom, I know it's my family in UK. Just call me Jayden or Jay, okay. I need a clean start'. Tiana felt insulted. 'How dare Tom refer to her as a new kid on the block? Who did he call a new kid? Who told him that she was on the block, let alone his block? This guy called Ron really had some guts', she thought in her mind.

Jayden continued talking 'Do you know Hubert Knight'? Tiana was startled. 'What's this'? She was hoping for a clean start and she had accepted her fate. She was looking forward to a new job and settling down in Nigeria. Someday, she would find the true love of her life. 'Err ..... yes Jayden, I do know Hubert Knight'. Was she expected to tell the world her story? She hesitated but when she saw the interest Jay showed in her response, she continued. She went on to tell of her nasty experience with Hubert; the guy that stringed her and stood her up in UK.

Jayden said 'I am Hubert Knight .... err .... I acted as err ….….. Hubert Knight …. No …. err …. Hubert Knight is a friend …. Emm I mean we are Hubert Knight …..err out…..Hubert Kni …...' Tiana was startled again and retorted 'What's this? Where is Reverend Iyanuloluwa? Is this a game'? The chaplain had promised to refer her for a job, now she was confronted with a maniac! Firstly he was Tom Freeman … then he became Ronald Bells ….. then he introduced himself as Jayden Freeman …..he is acting as Hubert Knight and then there are two Hubert Knight.

She was disgusted but tried to compose herself. She thought a job might be on the way for her. She asked quietly 'Tom …. Emmm Jayden are you alright'? Tom smiled reassuringly. Tiana comported herself once more and smiled and said in a low voice 'No sir, you aren't who I chatted with online and it's not your picture I saw. You are someone whose got his wires really crossed and in need of a break. Tell your business partners you need one. You obviously have got it all wrong somewhere and I don't play games'. She lost it and lashed out at Jayden.

PANSY'S CHEST

Jayden elucidated a bit more on Pansy to justify his actions. He said that as soon as Pansy became ill, the life of Fisher Empire began to go down too. The men that brought in large bags of money reduced drastically. Pansy's death led to the decline of the political and bubbly tone of the Chest. Pansy and her mother were the live wires of the politics and entertainment in the empire. They knew what to cook, what to say, where to get things and how to do things that made the political guys bring different currencies in large bags. On her death, the men stopped giving money completely and the empire had to rely on good spirited donors and the government. This motivated the management to introduce initiatives to generate income within the Chest.

Pansy then turned to him and said 'So that's my sponsor Pansy and her mother, Lady Mo. What has that got to do with Hubert Knight and the great deception in London? Did you and Pansy plan this? Were you both under the influence of drugs when you stalked me for a year and sent me to UK? What a spon ...'. Jayden interjected quickly, responding quietly he begged her to reduce the volume of her voice. He then informed her of how she came to be in the picture.

After Pansy's death in 2008, Don knew he needed company and also wanted to return to UK, yet he wanted to avoid Nigerian families. That was a tall order he placed so Don suggested he dated ladies in the orphanages. He had brought his attention to Tiana, another paragon of beauty. According to Jayden, he had planned the whole online dating arrangement with Hubert Knight to get to know her better. He was very paranoid of Nigeria so he couldn't approach her directly. He had been impressed firstly with her looks, then with her performance in the university and decided to send her to UK.

The original agreement was that once Tiana was settled in the Freeman's home in UK, he would make himself known to her, retire from Pansy's Chest and hand over to Hubert. Hubert shuttled between Nigeria and UK because his wife was based in UK but he made his own money from Nigeria. Hubert had been friends with Ron and had volunteered with different charities in Nigeria. His managerial experience was vaster than Ron's, so Ron recommended him for a more permanent post as an administrator with Pansy's Chest, when Ron left for UK.

Ron went on to declare that while his identity remained hidden after Pansy's death, he kept out of public eye to avoid being abducted by another Nigerian family. Although he was well taken care of in Pansy's Chest, he never anticipated that he would be introduced to a lifestyle of drugs and alcohol. He had controlled himself and had attempted to help Pansy do likewise, but lost the battle with her. His love for Pansy motivated him to stay on. Tiana remained silent.

He went ahead to inform her on the plan and attempt they had made to contact her. Jayden told Tiana that he fell in love with her immediately he saw her picture when she was still in the university. For security reasons and for fear he might be abducted again, he asked Hubert to fill in and act on his behalf. While he sent her the gifts and email directly; he stood beside Hubert whenever he chatted online. He told Hubert what to say and controlled the relationship. 'So why did

Hubert mess up'? Tiana asked.

Jayden explained that Hubert had to split up with her after she got to the bed and breakfast because he didn't want any physical contact with Tiana in UK. He had explained to Jayden that he was married with kids and didn't want any challenges with Tiana or his wife in UK. He had only enjoyed accompanying Ron in the mystery 'chase'. Hubert knew Tiana had seen him in pictures and through the video chats so he had to use someone else to get Tiana from the airport to the Freeman's home in Sanderstead. One of the boys employed to work on the Freeman's garden; Singh Raj was asked to prompt and program Tiana's moves till she got there.

Tiana responded 'So why did you not go through with your plans'? Jayden told her that the plan fell through when Singh couldn't get Tiana back to online dating. He had the mind to change back to his real identity online, reveal himself to her, inform his parents of his existence and join them in UK. Singh had reported to Hubert and Ron that Tiana said she didn't believe in online dating.

Tiana remembered meeting Singh at the bed and breakfast. He had been so chatty, friendly and helpful. Infact it was Singh that brought Tiana's attention to George and Rose Freeman at the bed and breakfast. He mentioned in passing that they supplied Croham Park bed and breakfast with dairy products. He also suggested to her that they might need help with cleaning their home and looking after the garden. It was armed with these leads that Tiana confidently approached the Freeman couple. She also remembered meeting Singh later in Freeman Garden. He worked as a farm manager and had helped her find her way round Sanderstead.

Tiana remembered that shortly after she settled into the Freeman's home, Singh had told her about online dating and tried to get her to go on it. She pretended that she didn't believe in it. She wasn't going to go online again. Never again! She had been so badly burnt and not even the tender hearted Singh would make her change her mind. He did all he could to link them together but she wasn't having another guy string her. She made Singh aware that while she looked up to him and admired him, she needed him to respect her boundaries.

Jayden said that got him disinterested and he knew that by the end of five years, Tiana would be asked to leave. He decided to wait till she returned to Nigeria. He took his mind off Tiana and concentrated on Pansy's Chest. Ron had no clue about the London team's visit nor did he know that there was a memorial service planned because they weren't part of the plan. Hubert didn't know either because he had stopped communicating with Singh as soon as Tiana warned him to desist from trying to get her involved with online dating.

Singh knew about the memorial service and other plans by the Freeman couple but he kept quiet because he didn't want to be involved with anything that would jeopardise his work. Tiana had privately threatened him with sexual harassment if he didn't desist from trying to get her back into online dating. Singh knew he could get into trouble with George and Rose too. He was only a farm manager and couldn't verify Tom's true identity. More so, he didn't want Tiana to return to Nigeria alone since she already told them how vulnerable she felt. Tiana asked 'So this was all masterminded by you and Hubert'? Jayden ashamedly nodded his head and apologised.

He told her that he still wanted the relationship, which was the purpose of the whole exercise. 'You are truly sick Tom', Tiana said. 'I am aware of that already, Miss Tiana Noire', Jayden responded. Tiana angrily stomped out of the chaplain's office. How was she expected to respond to what she had just heard? Surely, it was the devil on another assignment to waste her. Firstly it was Hubert Knight, now it's Tom Jayden. She had thought that they would at least offer her a job. As she stepped out of the chaplaincy to head back to the hotel, she bumped into the real Hubert Knight.

He was speaking with Reverend Iyanuloluwa and Reverend Olurantimi. She recognised him from the pictures he had exchanged with her online and the video chats they had been involved with. Tiana lost it. She screamed and ran out of the chaplaincy as fast as her legs could carry her. As she tried to cross the street to go back to the Glorious Hotel and Suites, she was brushed aside by a car. As she fell down, different thoughts flowed through her mind. 'How cruel can life be? Was life trying to return her to the bin where she came from? Definitely life didn't think she deserved to be treated with respect'.

Whilst she was on the floor, the two reverends appeared by her side with Hubert and Jayden, and a crowd followed behind. Up till then, everyone in the neighbourhood had seen Tiana moving together with white people. Now the white people were behind the two reverends and Tiana was on the floor after been brushed aside by a car. She wasn't watching when she hurried into the streets. Tiana's scream had attracted the crowd. As she bitterly wept, she said in a disappointing tone 'Reverend Olurantimi why, why, why? Why all these ….. Reverend Iyanuloluwa ……. you ….... you told me you were going to refer me for a job this morning. You …. You set me up. Why Reverend Why …… you are meant to protect the flock, not subject them to torture of the wolf ….. oh Reverend why'…….. I came back from London to get away from their mess', she sobbed. This embarrassed both reverends.

The reverends now had to calm her down and with the help of passers-by, they got her to a nearby clinic to have her checked out. All tests proved that she was okay, but for the minor bruises on her face and body. Reverend Iyanuloluwa excused himself to go for a program in church while Hubert and Ron walked behind Reverend Olurantimi. The three of them frantically apologised to Tiana, with the reverend emphasing that all he wanted was reconciliation. He reiterated that it was obvious Hubert and Jayden had carried out a wicked and selfish scheme and had not considered her emotions. Tiana had a right to press for charges for the emotional trauma they had caused her. If she charged them for impersonation and assault, she would be justified, but she needed to reconsider her stand as a godly person and embrace reconciliation.

At the clinic, Jayden went on his knees and apologised to Tiana. He had been satisfied with Tiana's conduct when they chatted online and while she was with his parents in Nigeria. This meant that she must have got along with them in UK and he wanted to take the relationship further. Hubert also apologised to Tiana, saying that it was all done with the best intention and stressed on how important it was to hide Tom Jayden's identity all those years. He said that Ron had been very paranoid after Pansy's demise.

The only picture she saw was Hubert's yet he had been a middle man for Jayden. She had fallen in love with two people thinking it was one. Tiana said 'Jayden how does that add up? You sure don't think I would suddenly love you because I lived and worked for your parents for five years or because you came up with a lame excuse of impersonation. You mean I was hearing your voice whilst looking at Hubert's pictures'? She apologised to the Reverend Olurantimi and said she was tired, needed some rest and privacy and had to return to her hotel room. He accepted the apology and regretted that neither himself nor Reverend Iyanuloluwa had helped her as promised but assured her that they would be of necessary help. Jayden then volunteered to take her to her hotel room in his car. She refused initially but as she felt faint, she had no choice but to accept the offer. Reverend Olurantimi and Hubert accompanied them.

Chapter Thirteen

The Breach

By the next morning, Tiana still felt weak and tired and requested for room service for breakfast. The room attendant brought in a tray of English breakfast of sausages, bacon, mushrooms, eggs and greens with wheat bread and green tea. She didn't realise how tired she was. She had just returned from UK and had led the London team to Nigeria for a memorial service. She had also been to OCHS where she grew up and Pansy's Chest; her benefactor's home.

Now she was confronted by Hubert and Jayden's morbid love tales. All she needed was a job when she was fully rested. She took almost two thousand pounds to UK five years ago and had been able to save almost three thousand five hundred pounds on departure. She hoped it would be able to support her as she got back into the Nigerian system.

After breakfast, she heard a knock on her door and wondered who it might be. It was a parcel containing a bouquet of flowers, some chocolates with a get well soon card from Jayden. She thanked the porter though she felt upset. She hardly knew the guy neither did she have any feelings for him. She began thinking about how to respond to Jayden's gesture and soon felt a slight headache. She took some paracetamol and drifted off to sleep. Her phone rang by twelve o'clock and it was Jayden. He had told her of his intention to come over to the hotel to see her but she told him it wasn't necessary. He insisted. He brought her some lunch and other items he felt would make her life easier in the hotel. She grudgingly told them at the reception to allow him into her hotel room after several minutes of deliberation.

In his hands were two large bags containing a large bouquet and two vases; which he set on her table. He also brought out a bottle of wine and two glasses and set them on her table. He presented her with a rose scented candle and a card to say 'sorry, I broke your heart'. She really wanted to tell him to take the items and leave but she was tired and hungry. The smell of the food in his bag made her hungrier. He had two portions of rice, salad and steak meat. Still in her pyjamas, Tiana reluctantly accepted the lunch. It was quite tasty. She then proceeded to take the analgesic given to her at the clinic. She lay on the bed and noticed how handsome Jayden was. As he spoke, she drifted off to sleep again.

She woke up to her alarm ringing, it was seven o'clock. At first she was confused. She was back from London. Yes. She was in the hotel room. Yes. There was a stranger in the room. Yes. It was Tom Jayden Freeman. What was he doing there and who let him in? 'Hello Princess Noire … Tiana Noire'. Tiana froze in her bed. No one had ever addressed her as Princess Noire, only Pansy. At least so she was told from the OCHS staff. They always referred to her as Tiana Ileaanuoluwakisu (in Nigeria) or Tiana Noire (UK). She liked the sound of the name Princess Noire. She then remembered she had opened her doors to Jayden that afternoon and they had lunch together. He had set the dinner table for two.

She felt much stronger on waking up and only the bruises on her face and body reminded her of the accident. The aroma from the dinner was very appealing and she recalled her dates when she was younger; Kolapo Andrews and Dandy Omojuola. She didn't even consider dating in UK. She had hoped that Hubert would turn up before the expiration of her permit to stay but that didn't happen. She had been badly bruised emotionally and had to concentrate on healing and getting her life back before returning to Nigeria. She also remembered the awards she got in school, as a girl not worthy of a man. She giggled.

She had been reminiscing on her past and not heard all Jayden said until he sat by her bedside. Then she got startled and he smiled. Her heart skipped a beat. 'I see you are miles away, fondling with some memories. Mind sharing the fun, mind putting a smile on my face or telling me what can make me giggle too'? She was still in her pyjamas. By then she felt dirty and sticky and decided to have a wash. After showering and dressing up, she sat at table and they both had dinner and quietly watched a movie together. About eleven o'clock later in the evening, the weather was cool outside and they both decided to go for a walk round the quiet streets.

While on their walk, Jayden told Tiana that although they met on an online dating site through Hubert, both of them knew her before the online meeting. He further enlightened Tiana on all he knew about her to reiterate his point. He informed her that Pansy sponsored a total of thirty children in OCHS, but only seven were taken there from infancy. Tiana had been the last new born baby taken there. After Tiana, the police had mounted up more vigilance in the area, to avoid future occurrences of babies being dropped by the bin. Tiana's case was the worst; she was just few hours old when she was found. If Pansy hadn't heard her cry after her political meeting, Tiana would have slept in the bin area all night, all covered in blood and hungry. It was likely that she might have died from infection too.

Jayden further said that although Pansy's Chest had no

contact with Tiana directly in accordance with their undertaking with OCHS, Pansy had monitored her through the support staff there. She often made reference to 'baby Noire the unusual baby' and was curious to know what she would become or who she would be. Despite Pansy's busy political lifestyle, she took time to follow up on her progress. Pansy had been overjoyed when she heard the bin baby Noire had gained admission to the university. She was also pleased that the six other babies she took to OCHS also progressed well into their respective callings.

For the first time, Pansy felt the love of a mother. Someone outside OCHS had monitored her progress. She felt bad that she had not gone to thank Pansy's Chest after her admission at the University, though she knew they had sponsored her. It was obviously too late to reciprocate the gesture because Pansy was late. While she was pondering on Pansy, Jayden informed her that the flat she had shared with her friends whilst at the university was owned by one of Pansy's friend.

Before Pansy passed away, she had asked her friend to

approach Habiba and offer her the accommodation at a discounted monthly rate. Tiana said that she remembered when Habiba presented them with the accommodation offer; the four friends agreed that it was a very good offer for the price. Tiana, Habiba and Chioma accepted it while Ewaoluwa opted to go to school from home. Then she said 'That didn't mean you should stalk me and send me off to UK to work on a farm, Tom …. Err Jayden'. He replied 'No, the background information is to make you aware of the effort that went into our plan before it was busted'.

Jayden further reminded her of an outing the ladies had while in school. The four friends had attended a bachelor's eve of one of Hubert's friends in Ikoyi. They were the only two white guys and they stayed in a quiet section of the house because the noise from the music set was too much for them. The four ladies had turned up as stunning as ever around eight o'clock in the night. They had been very bubby and chatty and had danced all night. Tiana recalled the bachelor party they all attended. Although she had attended few, the four friends had attended only one together. They had been invited by the bride who was the hair dresser on the ground floor in their block of flats in Yaba. Tiana never saw any white man there, though she remembered that there were a good number of people there and they were all in separate sections of the house, partying away.

Jayden said that after the party, Chioma met Hubert's wife; Kathy. She was a librarian at the British Council. Chioma went to find out how she could get her masters degree abroad on leaving school. In the course of her preparations, she became friends with Kathy. Jayden also met Chioma at the library and although he identified her as one of the four, he wasn't attracted to her. He noticed she was friends with Kathy and arranged with Hubert to introduce the four ladies to online dating. Jayden reminded Tiana of their online conversations with Hubert's pictures under his online profile. Tiana recalled the conversations. The descriptions actually matched Jayden's physical appearance, style of speaking and personality.

She also remembered that there were delayed responses to her online questions. It took Hubert a long time to respond to her questions during video calls. Jayden explained that during the video calls, Hubert had to pause for Jayden to respond to Tiana's questions. He sometimes wrote down the reply or made sign language which Hubert interpreted to Tiana. The response from the text messages and emails were quicker because they came from Jayden directly and got to Tiana faster. While they thought it was nice to get Tiana to his parent's house in Sanderstead, he was sorry that they had not factored in the psychological impact of the switch from Hubert to Jayden.

Although Hubert had made regular visits to London, he had avoided Tiana. Their plan was ruined when they couldn't get Tiana back onto the dating site. It was almost twelve midnight, when Tiana returned from the walk with Jayden. She had been too tired to respond to him. After the night walk, the tension between Tiana and Jayden had eased out and she felt she could warm up to him as a friend. What she didn't like was the fact that Jayden considered her because she was an orphan.

Chapter Fourteen

The Treasure In The Chest

The next day, a member of Reverend Iyanuloluwa's congregation put up an advert for the post of a health officer in Ikeja Health Clinic and the reverend recommended Tiana. The interview was slated for the week after so she could fully regain her strength and prepare for work. She planned to move out of her hotel accommodation and rent a place of her own once she was able to secure the job in Ikeja. Jayden called on Tiana later that same day in the hotel room. He was in Lagos for the week and would return to Pansy's Chest the following day. Jayden was very pleased to hear that Tiana would be attending a job interview the following week.

PANSY'S CHEST

They decided to go to The Conqueror Cinema Surulere. Since it was rebuilt after the Show Night, he had not been there. He and Pansy had narrowly escaped death about thirty years earlier. Now he was taking Tiana there to see the Lion King-Disney classic. Prior to the dance show, Jayden and Tiana had stopped at the restaurant for dinner. Reverend Olurantimi sighted them from the chaplaincy and nodded his head smiling.

This triggered Tom's memory of the Show Night. He had gone there with Tammie and other tourists. That was his first encounter with Pansy and she had been the angel sent from God, to guide him out of danger that night. He had woken up in Pansy's Chest the following morning. Coincidentally after the show with Tiana that evening, he would be in Pansy's Chest the next day. Thirty years ago he was a guest being treated; now he was a management staff helping others to recover.

After the musical show, Tiana and Jayden went back to her hotel room. He promised to keep in touch with her once he got to Pansy's Chest. Tiana knew she had to erase the image of Hubert and his ways off her mind and concentrate on Jayden. Although both men's images were on her mind, she knew Hubert was more handsome yet she preferred Jayden's personality. She struggled to get the image of Hubert out of her mind and only the pains and disappointments of her heart made her decide he wasn't worth considering. He was also married, so that was another safety net for her, she didn't fansy married men.

In the hotel, they sat down to have a glass of wine each. Then Jayden put on a soft classical music, dimmed the lights, turned on the candle and they both danced into the night. As their bodies touched each other, Jayden moved closer to Tiana and kissed her on the forehead. That was the first kiss she had since flirting with her third fling, Patrick Chike, the banker in Sagamu. She felt so tender as she allowed herself to be caressed by Jayden. Tension built in the room and soon they were making love passionately. She knew it was so wrong, yet she felt right. She was very angry yet she never wanted the night to end. Misery beclouded her yet she wasn't going to let go of the erotic moment. She had never been this close or intimate with a man. Tiana and Jayden had finally found romance in Pansy's Chest. Wednessday 3rd May, 2017.

By the time Tiana woke up the following morning, Jayden had left for Pansy's Chest. It was ten o'clock. He left a tray of English breakfast for her, two hundred and fifty thousand naira cash and a card that read 'thank you'. Once again Tiana thought to herself. 'What had she done? She had sex with a man she was just getting to know! This was against the christian doctrine.

In OCHS, Mother Pauline had emphasized the need for chastity till they got married. Tiana had broken her vow. Was she truly a success like Mother Pauline had presented her to the children? She had allowed herself to be disvirgined. Why Tiana why? Why had she cast off restrain? For twenty eight years, she had stood her ground, and now in a single night, a stranger had taken it all away. Was that why he left the thank you card'? She mockingly said to herself 'yeah Tiana Noire, thank you for a night of great sex. It was nice meeting you.

Have a good time in Nigeria. Next time be smarter'. Tiana was so full of remorse that she vowed she would never see Jayden again.

Four days elapsed since Tiana had sex with Jayden, yet no word from him. She felt used but she blamed herself for being so gullible. The stories of Hubert and Jayden were so convenient. All Jayden wanted to do was complete the work Hubert started. She had sex with him and he vanished. That was her payback to her sponsors. They probably did that to every lady they sponsored in OCHS. Vulnerable girls were their prey. They brought their sexual conduct from Fisher Empire to the girls that benefited from them. It was the turn of the bin baby Noire to be molested too! Her imaginations ran wild. 8th May 2017.

The phone rang and it was Jayden's number. That was the fifth time he was calling that day. She had been lost in her thoughts all the while. Her heart skipped a bit. She refused to pick the calls. She was preparing for her job interview the following day and didn't want another emotional roller coaster ride with Jayden. The pleasure was over, now she must build her life again, although she wasn't sure she could ever love or trust again. She had emptied herself online to men who didn't care, they had wasted five years of her life and one of them had just taken her virginity away and was trying to mess up with her entire life.

The job interview was a success and Tiana soon began work as a health officer at Ikeja Health Clinic. Her salary wasn't much so she had to look for a shared rented accommodation near the clinic. The money Jayden gave her was quite helpful but could not sustain her for a long period. Jayden rang her phone incessantly morning and evening but Tiana refused to pick his calls. He left messages to say he apologised for the sexual misconduct but she ignored his voice and text messages. She was done with him and ready to move on.

The skills Tiana had gained in UK had really helped her and everyone loved the new health officer in the clinic. She soon discovered that the health clinic had a way of assisting the staff having accommodation challenges. The staffs' rents were more economical if they took the accommodation jointly. Also the health officers who accepted the night shift and worked all night got cash incentives towards their accommodation from the clinic authorities. Tiana joined the shared accommodation scheme and also signed up to the night shifts arrangements. A week after she began work, she got a taxi to move her out of the hotel.

Tiana was returning to her flat after work one evening when she fainted at the entrance door of her home. They rushed her to the health centre and she got the worst news she had feared. She was pregnant. It had happened. Now her life was completely messed up. A new job with salary that was barely enough and a pregnancy. Life really had a way of acting up. Now Jayden had the gold medal for winning the relay race for her destruction. She was glad that she was out of his reach and that of the two reverends. She planned to work hard and look for ways of increasing her earning potentials.

The frequency of Jayden's phone calls and text messages had dropped drastically and she wouldn't dare to let him know that she was pregnant. What would he do? Ask her to abort and bade her farewell? Was he going to send her back to UK as a slave, never to be a bride? 'Miss Tiana Noire Anuoluwakishu'? She heard her name in the health centre. 'We would advise you to take it easy as you go home'. That was the last sentence she remembered the nurse saying as she left the clinic for her flat. She took the taxi home. 7th June 2017.

Chapter Fifteen

Free At Last!

Tiana's pregnancy was a difficult one in the first trimester. She spent more time at home than in the health centre. She was going to be a single mum and Jayden had stopped calling. As her pregnancy advanced, she became more beautiful and her ebony skin tone continued to glow with her blonde hair and hazel eyes. After a couple of weeks, her health gradually improved as she prepared for the baby's arrival. She was fortunate that Ikeja Health Clinic was twenty minutes walk from her shared accommodation. This was good exercise for her.

Her baby bump was very noticeable towards the middle of

the second trimester. All the while she had avoided Jayden and the two reverends. The Freeman couple had contacted her only once since they left for UK. They were glad to have met her, grateful for her role in their mission to Nigeria which led them to discovering their son and wished her well for the future. She was on her own and would never dream of telling them of her pregnancy. She must move on and face her life's choices.

In addition, Tiana's pregnancy meant that she couldn't afford to work very long hours so she cancelled her nightshifts arrangements and opted to run private home tutorials for children below the age of ten, in the evenings and at week ends. She got her pupils through the influence of Ewaoluwa who was a teacher. Her friends had been amazed at the turn of events in Tiana's life. They were angry at both Hubert and Jayden but Tiana's pregnancy left them confused. They felt that the only sensible thing that Tiana could do was to work hard, look after herself and prepare to cater for the unborn baby. They agreed that she didn't need Jayden in her life. They argued that if he ignored her for five years in UK that meant he wasn't serious.

Meanwhile Chioma got all she needed to study for her masters program in Birmingham, and her friends had a send off party for her. Habiba also met and fell in love with a project analyst at a business function; Khatumu Mansir. Their marriage took place on Saturday 7th October, 2017, a month after Chioma's departure in September. Ewaoluwa and Tiana helped with the event planning of Habiba's wedding. Ewaoluwa was the chief bridesmaid and Tiana had a more traditional role since she was heavily pregnant.

Back in her flat, Tiana heard a knock on the door on a Saturday evening after her last pupil had gone home. She opened it and standing between her and her big baby bump was Jayden. He looked very handsome but had a sad look on his face. He had few questions that needed to be answered. 'Why didn't she pick his calls or responded to his messages? Why didn't she tell him she was pregnant? Was the pregnancy for him? Did she find someone else and got pregnant for the person'? He stood starring at her as she blocked the door to the flat. She wasn't going to let him in. He brushed her aside, went in, grabbed her by the arm, dragged her in and shut the door behind them. He needed an explanation. Saturday 21st October 2017.

Tiana starred back at him speechless. Jayden moved closer to press Tiana's back against a wall. He began to kiss her and caress her. He told her that he had missed her and he looked forward to seeing her. Hubert had informed him of her pregnancy in the previous week. Chioma met up with Kathy in Birmingham and told her about Tiana's pregnancy.

Tiana was struggled to free herself from his grip but he held on tighter, with her back against a wall. She wanted to tell him to get lost but she needed his assistance. Her house rent was high, her fifty thousand naira a month salary wasn't great and she was going to have a baby soon. 'I said how far gone are you in your pregnancy Tiana, you seem to be in a faraway land'? Tiana remained silent. Jayden began to work all over her, caressing the baby bump and kissing her all over. He told her that he loved her and didn't come to cause her pain. He promised to be gentle with her and be by her side for the rest of his life and Tiana burst in tears.

She told Jayden that she didn't think his motives were truly right. She accused him of wanting an orphan to take to UK. He wanted someone without family so he can treat her anyhow. He didn't want to be accountable to anyone. She told him that she had repented and now belonged to the family of God and Mercy Chapel was her home and family. Jayden countered her accusation by admitting his mistake. That was the initial motive back then. Things had changed since her university days and a lot had happened between them. They have come to know more of each other since then too. He assured her that he would take care of her and she need not worry. It was going to be alright. If she let him in her life, she would never be alone again.

He promised to take her to see Reverend Iyanuloluwa and Reverend Olurantimi to repent and get their blessing before getting married in the registry. He also hinted that if her present rent was going to be an issue, she could quit her job and move into his pent house accommodation at Pansy's Chest. With time he would make travel arrangements for them to be back in Sanderstead.

On getting to Mercy Chapel, Reverend Iyanuloluwa was pleased to see the development that had taken place between Tiana and Jayden. He however expressed his dissatisfaction in them having pre marital sex and a baby outside wedlock. He told them that they had broken the commandment of the Lord. The couple repented and promised to fix a registry date before the end of Tiana's pregnancy. The reverend said the penitence prayer for them and they left.

Next the couple went to see Reverend Olurantimi in his house. He was with few members of the congregation from Mercy Chapel. The reverend asked to see them in his quiet room. He expressed his remorse at the couple for sleeping together before being married. According to him, westernisation was not an excuse for infidelity. He expected more from Tiana, seeing she had been a Sunday school teacher. The couple apologised and said they had repented and gone to see Reverend Iyanuloluwa, who prayed for them.

Jayden added that they came to see Reverend Olurantimi so he could bless their union too. Tiana said it was important for her to have the Nigerian father's blessings, since she didn't know who her parents were. Reverend Olurantimi blessed them both and led them back to his living room where the other members of the congregation sat. That was when Jayden and Tiana learnt that Reverend Olurantimi was getting married to Eunice Ireadale in three weeks.

It had been a delight to see the reverend. That would be his first wedding at seventy four years old and Eunice was fifty three. He never had a real date after Lady Mo Fisher; neither did he have any child after Pansy. He expressed hope in God and believed that he and Sister Eunice would have children after marriage. He had joined multitudes of people together in holy matrimony in different parishes around the country and had christened many babies too. Yet it never occurred to him that God would give him a life partner till he met Sister Eunice. He always blamed it on his carelessness with Pansy

PANSY'S CHEST

and her mother.

The people that knew him and lady Mo while Pansy was visiting him at his various priestly posts were his source of support. He hardly mentioned anything to the people he met after Pansy stopped visiting. He became silent on his private life when Pansy forsook him and adopted a prodigal lifestyle. He never knew or heard about Jayden Freeman; the son in-law that never was.

The reverend confessed that on hearing Jayden's account with his daughter, he was full of animosity initially. It took the grace of God and faith to come to terms with it and be at peace with him. They had both dealt in drugs and alcohol, and while Jayden came out clean, his only daughter had died. He expected more from him. He felt Jayden should have had the courtesy to get in touch with him if he really wanted to help Pansy. He was sure that Pansy must have told him that her father was a priest. More so, it was Pansy's Chest that communicated her death to him through the solicitors. This was well after she was buried.

PANSY'S CHEST

Jayden said that he was sorry that the reverend felt that way or had his own expectations of how things ought to have been. He explained that it was Pansy's wish for them to stay away from him. She felt she had let her father down but wanted them to assure him of her salvation. She didn't want him to see her deteriorated body, but preferred him to remember the little Pansy that always visited him, attended bible studies with him and went on evangelism with him. She wanted him to remember her as the bubbly pretty daughter that was always at the entrance gate to the church vineyard, welcoming guests, when they held bazaar at adult's annual harvest in church.

Though he felt sad at the turn of event with his daughter, Reverend Olurantimi said he was glad Pansy repented before she died. He said that he had forgiven them both, Pansy had passed away nine years earlier and as expected, Jayden had moved on with his life. His had made a choice to marry Tiana and he wished them well. He was also pleased that Pansy had impacted people's lives in her life time.

PANSY'S CHEST

He also said that Tiana made him very proud of his daughter Pansy. This was the reason he was in support of full reconciliation between Tiana and Jayden. Life had not been fair, but the hand of God had been evident in the reverend's ministry experience and personal life. Now he would be marrying Sister Eunice and like biblical Abraham, he trusted God for children.

Eunice had connected with the reverend when she learnt about Pansy; her life and death. It was easy for her to connect because she had lost her only daughter, Sandra in the Show Night too. More so, she was the only one who really took out time to minister to his needs after the meetings he held with the London team. His other guests had gone to their various homes or hotel rooms. Neither Jayden nor Tiana had noticed any development between them until they bumped into her in the reverend's house. The whole church and neighbourhood community knew about the reverend's relationship but Tiana and Jayden had been lost in their own world in Ikeja. The couple were glad for the reverend and promised to be at his wedding.

PANSY'S CHEST

Reverend Olurantimi was getting married! What a shock. He had been confined to the ministry for so long no one thought he would ever get married. Most people thought he had embraced celibacy and had got used to him. He was a member of every home at every parish he served as priests. His followers made room for him anytime he popped in or had a need. Even Pansy's mum had ensured he had his own building before she passed on. Not only were Reverend Olurantimi's sermons powerful, he also had the gift of healing. Reverend Olurantimi was known among the christian community in Nigeria. If he wasn't laying hands on people at the chaplaincy, he was busy ministering to people in his home or in their homes.

The Freeman couple never knew that their decision to come to Nigeria would produce so much effect. Firstly they discovered their son was still alive and was trying to get back home. Next Tiana solved the mystery of her travel to UK, and was now rightfully with her partner. Then through the meeting of the families of the victims of the Show Night, Reverend Olurantimi was going to get married to Sister Eunice Ireadale.

Chapter Sixteen

Awakened From The Nightmare.

The wedding ceremony between Reverend Olurantimi and Eunice Ireadale was a very successful one in Mercy Chapel. It was well attended by guests from all over the country and Reverend Iyanuloluwa officiated. It was also graced by the presence of Claudia's parents, Olufemifunre and Motolawo Oluwaloju. The London Team; Sammy Godwin, Tricia Warren and Zelda Topping sent monetary gifts of two hundred pounds to the reverend and his wife. The Freeman family sent the couple a wedding gift of two return tickets to UK. They were also invited to stay in Freeman Home and Garden for a month before returning to Nigeria. Saturday, 11th November 2017.

PANSY'S CHEST

George and Rose had been very grateful that their son Tom Jayden was still alive and had been blessed by the ministry of Reverend Olurantimi during their visit to Nigeria. At the request of Tiana and Jayden, the two reverends were asked to remain silent on Tiana's pregnancy and the couple's registry wedding. It would be a surprise for George and Rose Freeman when the couple got to Sanderstead.

The reverend was very grateful for the tickets and agreed that there was no need for George and Rose to attend their wedding in Nigeria. The gift was a much welcomed one, since he had never visited the UK. More so Jayden couldn't afford his parent's maintenance if they came to Nigeria for the reverend's wedding because he needed to save enough money to return with Tiana to UK and support their baby on arrival.

About a month after the reverend's wedding, Jayden took Tiana to Ikoyi registry and the couple held a small reception for their friends. This was also their farewell party. Jayden had handed over his role in Pansy's Chest to Hubert as planned. Prior to that, Jayden had informed Reverend

PANSY'S CHEST

Olurantimi of his succession plan to hand over his office to Hubert. They made a private arrangement to keep the post for foreigners, so they could help secure foreign aid, in times of distress. This ensured that the foreigners were comfortable, working in Nigeria. The clergy of Mercy Chapel was encouraged to minister in Pansy's Chest and another door was opened to them to minister in OCHS too. Saturday 16th December, 2017.

Pansy's Chest had offered so many gifts to people. It met the political needs of the people, sponsored children in orphanages, helped in rehabilitating Pansy and other drug addicts. The support team also helped in re integrating the victims back into the society. Once a volunteer in Pansy's Chest, Hubert now had a permanent position as an administrator. Ministry doors opened up to Mercy Chapel in Pansy's Chest. Tiana was the trophy Tom Jayden (Ronald Bells) got for his service in Pansy's Chest. She was good enough for UK. Jayden was the treasure Tiana found in Pansy's Chest, as she sought for information on her benefactor.

PANSY'S CHEST

Although Tiana had been glad to see Hubert in Nigeria, the attraction vanished when she heard the truth behind their romance. Between Hubert and Jayden, her integrity, dignity and emotional wellbeing had being compromised through their wicked schemes. The extent of the damage could only be rectified through a corrective measure that promised to protect her uncompromisingly and support her wellbeing as she embraced an unknown future.

With disappointments over and hurts subsided, Tiana had to move on and embrace the future with Jayden. Now she was married to Jayden, would she learn to love him for the rest of her life? This relationship had been a by product of dating over the internet for a year before she left for UK. She went to explore her world with her lover and was conquered. She returned to Nigeria and became a conqueror. Within few months of her return, she was engaged to be married and also expecting her first child. The battle that was lost in UK was eventually won in Nigeria. For the future, she hoped the relationship with Jayden worked out fine because the last five years had been a terrible roller coaster ride emotionally. She had just woken up from a terrible nightmare.

Tiana knew that she would be living with George and Rose in the Freeman Home and Garden upon their arrival in the UK so she planned to help out, like she had done in her previous trip. She wasn't aware of the current state or happenings with the Freeman couple because she had agreed with Jayden to keep away from them till they got to UK. Tiana was aware of the consequence of their actions in the British culture but Jayden promised to take charge of the whole process. He was going back to his parents' home after thirty years so he had to thread carefully. He didn't want to embarrass them or inconvenience his parents with his new family so he had to think of a re-integration plan that would work well for all concerned.

Since his reconnection with his parents in Nigeria in 2017, Tom Jayden kept in regular touch with them through the social media network and the phone. He told them so much about his life but was silent on Tiana and her unborn baby. When asked he told them that he would try and settle down with a lady on his return to the United Kingdom. His father told him the cottage was still as big as ever and there was room for him to come back and live with them. George informed him of the tremendous development that had taken place in Sanderstead since he left over thirty years ago. Sanderstead had opened up to modernisation and was a developing community. He reassured Jayden that he would definitely fit in easily.

George also updated him on the neighbour's activities. The Jacks upon their retirement ten years ago opened and ran a care home from their cottage called Jack + Sons. This was similar to the one Dora was kept in Riddlesdown. Jayden suggested to his parents that Dora be moved to Jack + Sons. He said that he would make enquiries on the possibilities of moving her there and also the likelihood of him volunteering there on his return to UK. He had been away for a very long time, and that was one of the easiest ways of getting back into the system. More so, it meant that Dora would be closer to home and the Freeman family could be together finally.

PANSY'S CHEST

Rose and George were very delighted. George suggested that Jayden speak with the Jacks, seeing Jayden had some experience as an administrator with Pansy's Chest in Nigeria. Jayden took their details and promised to get in touch with them.

The seventy three year old Fraser Jack was the consultant director and doctor at Jack + Sons and his wife Kathryn assisted him. They placed their four sons Xavier, Ethan, Jordan and Denzel in strategic management positions to support them. Jayden contacted Fraser and introduced himself to him. The Jack family were delighted and relieved that Tom was still alive. They knew George and Rose went to Nigeria for his memorial service but returned to give them the good news of his narrow escape from the hands of death. Jayden then informed Dr Fraser of his proposal to have Dora transferred to Jack + Sons from Riddlesdown.

Dr Fraser informed Kathryn of Jayden's proposal. He also mentioned Jayden's intention to return to the Freeman Home and Garden to live with his parents. He had been an administrator for a care home and drug rehabilitation centre in Nigeria and had proposed to volunteer in Jack + Sons Home. They both ran the idea by their children who decided to speak with Jayden first, investigate what he had been up before making the decision.

The Jack family held a couple of online meetings with Jayden and his references to conduct an investigation on his professional life in Nigeria. They were happy with their findings and proceeded to contact George and Rose. The Freeman couple was happy with the turn out of events and promised to give their full support in ensuring Dora was successfully transferred to Jack + Sons. Dr Xavier Jack contacted Jayden and informed him that the Jacks had welcomed the idea of transferring Dora to their care home and also had offered to give Jayden the opportunity to work as a volunteer care worker upon his return to Sanderstead. Xavier was a consultant neurosurgeon and the eldest child of Dr Fraser Jack; he ran the home under his parent's supervision. Between the Freeman family in UK and the Jacks, Dora was eventually moved to Jack + Sons.

Chapter Seventeen

A New Dawn

The effect of moving Dora closer home had its consequences on the Freeman household. They had to reschedule their plans to include visiting Dora more often. On their return to Sanderstead from their mission to Nigeria, the void left by Tiana was so great that they employed a thirty five year old Spanish live in house keeper, Dahlia Monk.

Rose asked Dahlia to prepare the room for Jayden's arrival; the stage was set for Jayden's return. He had informed his parents that he would be coming with his friend Hubert, who shuttled between UK and Nigeria. He would be pivotal in helping Jayden settle back into the system.

PANSY'S CHEST

Tiana vowed to emulate Pansy in her charity deeds when she got to UK. In the midst of her muddled life, Pansy had blessed so many. Unlike Pansy with an affluent background, loving and caring family, delinquent lifestyle but a godly ending, Tiana's story was so different. Her life had been the tale of a thrash picked at the garbage bin in Sagamu, refined and sent forth as a slave in Sanderstead, rejected and thrust back to Nigeria as a dejected lady. She was now headed for a wifely role in Sanderstead, full of anxiety for the future. She was extremely grateful to her three friends Chioma, Ewaoluwa and Habiba who stood by her.

The nightmare was over and out of the four friends; Ewaoluwa was the only one left unmarried. Habiba got married in Nigeria and Chioma got engaged whilst on her masters program in UK. Tiana then planned to set Ewaoluwa up with one of the men working in the Freeman Garden. The Indian man, Singh Raj had been very supportive to Tiana whilst she was in UK. On getting to UK, Tiana would encourage Singh to date Ewaoluwa. She hoped that the friendship would lead to marriage.

PANSY'S CHEST

Tiana's travel experience to UK was better because Jayden was beside her. It was her third time on the plane but that didn't calm her travel nerves. She still found the take off and landing nauseating. The couple had to give more than half of their belongings away, as they finally relocated to UK. Jayden had previously sent their remaining luggage from Nigeria by cargo and that was expected to arrive in UK in a forth night. This time around, Jayden called a black cab to take them from Gatwick Airport to Sanderstead. They had six pieces of heavy luggage to carry.

Upon arrival at the Freeman home, Dahlia opened the door to receive Jayden and Tiana. She introduced herself and led them through the lobby of the cottage over to the living room where Rose listened to the radio. It was ten o'clock in the morning. George sat next to Rose where they were both waiting for Tom and Hubert. On seeing Jayden, Rose was ecstatic, screamed, jumped out of her seat and embraced him. She hadn't taken note of his escort. George on the other hand passed out on his seat on seeing Tiana heavily pregnant. Dahlia rushed over to his side to resuscitate him.

PANSY'S CHEST

When George came round, he had mixed feelings. He knew he had been mischievous as a child, but Tom was proving to be more mischievous with each passing day. George recalled that when Jayden had told his parents he was coming to UK with a guest, they were expecting Hubert. They weren't expecting it to be his fiancé and they definitely weren't expecting Tiana. They never sensed anything between the two of them in Nigeria. Tom apologised and said he wanted it to be their surprise.

Jayden smiled to himself as he remembered how he had engaged Hubert, Kathy and Singh to play the impersonation game. They hid Tiana's identity until the couple arrived at the Freeman Home. Rose on the other hand, was pleased to see Tiana again. Although she was shocked at the turn of events between Tiana and Tom, she was too delighted at the return of her son. It was with great joy she welcomed the couple.

After lunch, Jayden took Tiana to the neighbour's cottage next door. Jordan was around to welcome Tom Jayden. He was the manager on duty. They weren't expecting Jayden that afternoon. The agreement was that Jayden would come in to see the management of Jack + Sons Home, on arrival in Sanderstead. Although they had promised him a volunteering role, he had to come and sign an agreement form of competence when he got in.

Jayden introduced Tiana to Jordan who expressed his joy and admiration for him when he saw Tiana. The Jacks never knew Tom Jayden was married; he had been discreet about his relationship. Jordan was silently grateful that they had insisted on seeing Jayden before offering him the volunteering role. How many more things were they going to discover about Tom Jayden? They knew Tiana had worked initially as a house keeper before becoming a home and garden administrator for Freeman home and Garden, they never expected that she would one day be Tom Jayden's fiancée.

Jayden told Jordan he was there to visit Dora but Jordan suggested he paid a courtesy call on his parents first. Jordan led the couple to his parents. Although they were shocked to see both Jayden and Tiana, they said they were overjoyed that

Jayden had done well for himself in finding a life partner. Fraser and Kathryn though shocked, congratulated the couple and promised to invite them over for dinner once the couple settled down. Jordan took Tom and Tiana to the ward where Dora was housed.

As Tiana and Jayden's church wedding approached, she got in touch with Chioma who was studying for her Association of Chartered Certified Accountant (ACCA) program in Birmingham. Chioma got excited and planned a surprise bridal shower for her on the night of the eve of her wedding. Reverend Olurantimi and his wife Eunice also planned their holiday visit to London to coincide with Tiana's wedding. They arrived the week before the wedding. With the permission of Jayden and his parents, Tiana invited Chioma to help out at home, in the week running up to her wedding. Hence the Freeman had a full house.

On the eve of their church wedding, the male staff in Jack + Sons Home and Jayden's few friends went over to Croham Park to celebrate his bachelor's eve party. While Jayden was away, the Freeman family retreated to their quiet corners. Chioma suggested that she and Tiana chat with Habiba and Ewaoluwa. In the video conference, both Ewaoluwa and Habiba sent their best wishes to Tiana. It was then that Habiba welcomed Tiana to her surprise bridal shower online. Habiba explained that since Tiana was heavily pregnant and had just arrived in UK, the three friends had gathered to cheer her up quietly on the eve of her wedding to Jayden. The three friends all wore peach laced up dresses bought by Chioma. She had sent the clothes to Habiba and Ewaoluwa in Nigeria. The bridal shower had caught Tiana unawares.

Chioma presented Tiana with a card and a book-set on animal farming for her wedding gift. It was on behalf of the three ladies and their families. There were twelve books in the set. Tiana was shocked on opening it and looked puzzled but Chioma encouraged her by saying she needed to get educated on animal farming, seeing that was the Freeman's family trade. The four friends burst out laughing as Chioma opened a bottle of non alcoholic wine. Habiba and Ewaoluwa also opened similar bottle of wine to toast to the occasion online.

PANSY'S CHEST

The four friends chatted away into the night, drinking as they spoke about everything from advise for the 'about to wed' bride to managing a marriage to make it endure stormy seasons. The internet session came to an end at about two o'clock in the morning and the ladies all went to bed.

Jayden and Tiana got married at the Parish Church Saint James Riddlesdown on Saturday 6th January 2018 and Chioma was the chief bride's maid. In attendance were the staffs at Freeman's Home and Garden and Jack + Sons Home. They chose winter farmhouse as their wedding theme so the animals in the garden could feature. It was a glamorous occasion and the wedding reception was held in the Freeman Garden, under a large marquee. The other members of the London team; Sammy Godwin, Tricia Warren and Zelda Topping came with their spouses. Reverend Olurantimi and his wife were really impressed with the wedding. It was so different to the weddings he had officiated or witnessed in Nigeria. He eventually left with his wife for Nigeria after their one month's visit.

PANSY'S CHEST

Three weeks after the wedding, in the mid hours of the morning, Tiana felt a sharp pain in her stomach, her water broke. She beckoned over to Jayden as he slept next to her. He hurriedly got up and reached for her already packed maternity bag. He took her to the hospital and by five o'clock in the evening and Tiana was delivered of a set of twins a boy and a girl. They had wanted the twin birth to be a surprise to all, so they kept it a secret. Monday, 12th February 2018.

The children cried a great deal on arrival and were given to Tiana in turn to feed; after they had been cleaned. For the first time, Tiana had a glimpse of her birth circumstances. How could a woman go through such an ordeal of child birth and still end up dumping her baby by the bin? At least her mother should have taken her to Oluremilekun Children's Home herself or a similar orphanage. Maybe she didn't have the money! Tiana thanked God Pansy came along.

Jayden had been around throughout the birth of the twins and it had been a horrific but exciting experience for him. On seeing them, Jayden got so excited and he thought they were the most beautiful babies in the world. He suddenly remembered Pansy Jere Fisher, way back in Nigeria. She was not only a very beautiful lady; she had been the most beautiful thing that happened to him throughout their life together. For a moment he was saddened at the loss of Pansy and the life he had shared with her. At the cries of the twins, he refocused his mind on the present. He looked at Tiana and the children. Tiana was more beautiful, darker and taller than Pansy, with overpowering hazel eyes and beautiful blonde hair. She was simply irresistible.

Tiana was the princess that consoled him and crowned him with love after Pansy's death. The twins looked so adorable too. Unlike Tiana, they were both fair skinned and had the same blonde hair and hazel eyes as their mother. Jayden hoped they turned out as glamorous and generous as Pansy but as humble and godly as their mother Tiana. He still found it hard to get Pansy out of his mind. What was it about her? Pansy! That is the name of a hybrid plant cultivated in the garden; it gave off beautiful aroma at dawn and at dusk and also made good salads. This was the effect Pansy Jere Fisher had on his life in Nigeria. She had fragranced his life in Nigeria, fed him and cared for him; Tiana and the twins were the by products he brought back to UK.

Prior to the birth of the twins, Tiana had shown signs of being jealous of his relationship to the late Pansy and he wasn't going to trigger her by naming his twins Pansy or a hybrid of Pansy. He secretly wanted to keep the Nigerian tradition of naming children after events, so he decided to name his children after the flowers he admired most; Chrysanthemum and Marigold. He mentioned this to Tiana and they both agreed that the Freeman twins would be called Chrysanthemum Jayden–Freeman and Marigold Jayden-Freeman respectively.

George and Rose went to the hospital to see Jayden and his new family. They expressed their shock at the news of the arrival of the twin because they were expecting one baby. George told Jayden that he refused to pass out and was prepared for more pranks. He hoped Chrysan and Marie wouldn't be as mischievous as Tom. Rose chuckled and said it seemed the Freeman family had adopted the names of flowers. She was the Rose of the family and had employed Dahlia to be the family's house keeper. Now Tiana had given birth to a set of twins and Tom had named them after beautiful flowers. This was a good omen for Freeman Home and Gardens.

The arrival of the twins kept Tiana very busy and as they grew within the first few months, Tiana got the inspiration to set up a nursery to take care of children under five. She met another couple who shared the same interest and decided to have a partnership arrangement with them. This would also help her look after her own twins. Although she wanted to work as a healthcare officer for adult or children, she and Jayden had agreed that she would do that later on, when the children were off to high school. She was grateful for the childcare training she had received during her previous trip to UK and the teaching experience she had in Nigeria as she taught private students referred to her by Ewaoluwa. She planned to apply her knowledge of child health care into her nursery. She would also plan to have an excellent health care and first aid service for the children in the nursery.

Rita, her children's nanny thought it was a good idea and promised to support her. She ran the idea by Jayden. He also felt it was a good idea and a way to be independent of his parents and the Home and Garden. They both began to work on a business proposal to start a nursery with the Littlewoods. Dahlia was already satisfying the role of a house keeper, and they needed to employ a new nanny to replace Rita. Rita would then help Tiana with the set up and running of the nursery. After the twins' first birthday, she would be set up a nursery to cater for children under fives.

As the twins grow and become more independent, she would extend the age bracket to year six. Rita recommended her Irish friend to replace her. It was twenty year old Alannah who was searching for a nanny role. Both Jayden and Tiana welcomed the idea of having her replace Rita once they started running the nursery. They would get additional help later.

Seven months after the birth of the twins the Freeman family received an email from Reverend Olurantimi that Sister Eunice had delivered quadruplets; two girls and two boys through IVF treatment. It had always been Reverend Olurantimi Omoba - Asejere's desires since they got married to have children. He called them Ope Omoba–Asekun Asejere, Iyin Omoba- Asepe Asejere and Ola Omoba-Aseyori Asejere and Ayo Omoba-Asela Asejere. The reverend said that was his life's testimony. God had profited him by making his work whole, complete victorious and an overcomer.

The reverend told the Freeman family that he wept for joy when he heard the news. He was on a peace keeping mission to the northern part of Nigeria. Some members of his congregation were sent to help set up a school on their newly acquired property in the north. The members had formed a house fellowship to meet and pray regularly for the success of the project. The house group soon gained popularity and seemed to be succeeding and attracting a crowd.

Some youths in the region saw the development and decided to traumatise the members and made it difficult for them to function properly. They felt they were forming a church, and making lots of money from people but overlooking the depravity of the area. Mercy Chapel continued to pray and look for a way to reconcile with the youths so the church project can be a success and there can be peace in the area. It appeared the youths didn't realise that what they saw were the effects of charity donations from privileged members of the church who worked across the country.

The chapel then decided to host the youths to a series of constructive youth development programs. They ran a series of christian programs on camp sites in different villages to appease the youths in the area. They also helped raise funds from the south to help support less privileged youths and motivate them to work. Through this means, a number of the youths got converted to Christianity. It was towards the end of the year long program that the reverend received the news of the birth of his children.

Sister Eunice had been overjoyed at the birth of the children. Throughout her pregnancy, she also had been very faithful in her service. She supported the youth counsellors and Sunday school teachers. She had a very good soprano voice so she joined the volunteer singers. Since she married the reverend, the choir had released about six praise and hymn albums and all the proceeds were donated to charitable causes.

However Sister Eunice could not feed the babies herself so members of the congregation took turns in helping with the feeding using baby bottles. There were also donations from church members from all over the country. Habiba and Khatumu brought suitcases of baby clothes while Ewaoluwa brought boxes of baby toys. The two ladies volunteered to help Sister Eunice with her shopping regularly and the Freeman family raised a donation of two hundred pounds on behalf of the London Team.

About The Author

Christiana .T. Moronfolu is firstly an aspiring architect then an author. She had her training at Yaba College of Technology (2000) before proceeding to London South Bank University (2013). She later had her masters in Construction Project Management from same university (2015). While on temporary career breaks, she diverts her energy to private studies and also writing. She has added two novels, 'Pansy's Chest' (2018) and 'Love On Seperate Grounds' (2018) to her existing collections; Destiny's Garden (2012) and Destiny's Fight (2012). Through her writings, she hopes to inspire, inform, entertain, admonish, encourage and celebrate her readers.

She left the shores of Nigeria to meet her fiancé in UK, but faced an embarrassing situation. The man she taught she knew didn't exist. Did the future hold any promise for Tiana Noire Ileanuoluwakishu, a lady with an inglorious background?

He had been faced with wealth, power and a lady with a heart of gold. Can Jayden get rid of the drugs and settle for a happy ending with the love of his life in Nigeria? There had been a memorial service to commemorate the nasty demise of loved ones. In the midst of tears and anger, could this memorial service be the start of joyous events? What is in the Chest?

Pansy's Chest is a fiction novel set in the present dispensation to unveil the dilemma of love and real life issues.